# Love at Frost Sight

## A HOLIDAY NOVELLA

### TORIE JEAN

**SUNSET AND CAMDEN CREATIVE**

This book is a work of fiction. Names, characters, places, and incidents are either products of the author's imagination or used fictitiously. Any resemblance to actual events, places, or person, living or dead, is entirely coincidental and not intended by the author.

LOVE AT FROST SIGHT

TORIE JEAN

Print ISBN: 9798218145545

For information on subsidiary rights, please contact the author at www.toriejean.com

Copyright © 2023 by Torie Jean

Cover design: Torie Jean

Copy Editing: Kristen Hamilton at Kristen's Red Pen

All rights reserved. No portion of this book may be reproduced, distributed, or transmitted in any form or by any means, including information storage and retrieval systems, without prior written permission from the publisher or author, except for the use of brief quotations in a book review or post.

*Adam,*
*"This page, in fact, this book is dedicated to you."*
*I'm still bitter that you killed cloud factories for me,*
*but because of you, I believe in faerie tales.*

*Thank you for being my soulmate.*

# author's note and trigger and content warnings:

Oh, well, hi, there!

Thank you so much for picking up this winter novella. I appreciate you so so so so much.

Before we get going, here are a few things to keep in mind. If something doesn't sound to your taste or might be triggering to you, remember mental health first always! Put this down and find something else. It'll be here if/when you're ready. No hard feelings.

Like me, Maddie has a disease called endometriosis. Endometriosis is a chronic illness where tissue similar to the lining in the uterus grows wherever it wants throughout the body. This disease is both painful and chronic, so while this is a silly love story, for some, that aspect may be heavy. Please keep in mind that millions of people live with this disease daily; as one of those people, those elements are my life. In the end, you do you, boo!

*Love at Frost Sight* has fantastical elements that require the reader to suspend their disbelief a smidge. It's a project I did to get me through some doctors' appointments, and the story doesn't take itself too seriously. Still, I hope it can be a bit of a happy escape for y'all.

Content and Trigger Warnings:

**Love at Frost Sight contains:**

- Endometriosis representation which includes significant pain, taking narcotics, isolation of hiding a chronic illness, interactions with ableism, off-page vomiting, difficulty with intimacy, and nausea.
- A character with an anxiety disorder
- An accident between a pedestrian and a car that happened in the past
- Manipulation and bullying
- History of neglectful and abandoning parental units

**This book also contains the following:**

- On-page intimate scenes, including fingering, oral, and penetrative sex.
- Adult language. If you would rather not read swear words, this one will not be for you.

# CHAPTER ONE
## The Shop Around the Corner
### MADDIE

"YOU'RE THE VILLAIN, RIGHT?" A pair of feline eyes narrow on my face, unflinching behind the weathered pine counter of this bookstore my boyfriend Connor and I wandered into. Thick bifocals slope down the store clerk's turned-up nose, obscuring the unnatural chartreuse hue of her stare, unblinking and unsettling in its assessment of me, as if she's seen past the outward appearance I've put so much effort into perfecting, straight into my soul where I've buried Marshmallow Maddie Finch as deep as she will go.

Nervously, I shift my weight onto my opposite foot and stare at the dusty floorboards. People seeing the regrettably soft part of me is something I avoid at all costs.

With a collecting breath, I dig my long nails into my palms, grounding myself in our stand-off. The first rule of Mean Girl Fight Club is not to let on that you're bothered.

I am calm. I am cool. I am collected.

I should stop staring at the ground.

Lifting my gaze, I meet her eyes, and a kaleidoscope of repeating patterns swirls enchantingly within her stare instead of the previous scrutinizing glare.

"Girl, I said—you're the villain, right?" Ellie, if the nametag pinned to her cardigan covered in garland and jingle bells is to be trusted, drums her fingers against the dated countertop, waiting for an answer to what I assumed was a rhetorical question.

"Excuse me?" I ask. Maybe I didn't hear her right over the whir of the table fans rescuing us from a late-summer-like heat wave.

Ah, winter in Texas.

Hot. Demoralizing. Suffocating.

Gorgeous.

A time where, if it wasn't for the mammoth Christmas tree dominating every outdoor shopping center and Wham's *Last Christmas* whining over this store's speaker, I could ignore the nauseating merry hell December promises to be.

"No. No. That's not right. You weren't supposed to be," she says with a twitch of her snub nose and a narrow of her cat eyes to slits. "You reek of Jack."

And wow. Okay, Madeline. Time to move away from the eccentric bookstore owner before you're stabbed. This isn't a contest worth winning.

I hazard a glance around the store, searching for Connor, the man responsible for my unfortunate presence here on an otherwise perfect Sunday. Imposing bookshelves loom overhead, filled to the brim with jewel-colored tomes, obscuring my sight line and Connor's presence. With a sigh, I accept my fate. I don't trust giving Ellie my back when she's primed for a lunge and murder scenario, so this conversation, however irritating, will have to continue.

"No offense," I say, with laser-focused attention on my nails. "But are you sure you're not smelling whiskey on your breath?"

"Not Jack Daniels, girl." Ellie slams her hand down on the counter. Change rattles with the drub. I jump—my pulse skitters. The whole commotion is unnecessary. "Jack Frost. He thinks he's being clever with his spite when he ruins one of my carefully crafted stories. But you're the one paying, having a heart of frost in someone else's tale when you should have a beautiful story of love and healing all your own." She shakes her head. The glass bead chain hanging on the edge of her eyewear catches the light streaming in from the window and a rainbow cascades like a sparkling mirrorball along the wall. It's far too brilliant of a light show to be cast from such an ordinary object. My stomach twists again. This isn't a normal conversation with an unhinged, burnt-out retail worker around the holidays.

My ex-best friend Jenny would say it's because Ellie is clearly fae. Jenny had this theory—well, she had lots of bonkers ideas—but the one she clung voraciously to is that this world hovers near a faerie realm. On Halloween, we enter each other's orbit, when all the fae are free to play without anyone noticing, and stay through the New Year when the orbits move off each other's path. *That's why it always feels so magical after Halloween.* But her bizarre theory is one of the many reasons we're no longer friends, so I won't humor it now.

"Oh, Jack. Are you happy? Her mate is near, and their timing is all wrong." She tsks, with her head in a solemn bow.

The antique hardwood floor groans as I step back on my heels. I'm unsure whom Ellie is conversing with since it's not me, and Connor is the only other person in the store.

"Never mind!" she continues, oblivious to my deliberate, creeping retreat. Or maybe she doesn't care. It's not like I'm providing much to this unusual tête-à-tête. "I know what I'll do! Rewrite! Yes! A holiday one, while there's time! Don't want to waste a match like yours. It was one of my favorites in this town." She reaches behind her head, plucking a pencil from her bun. Blonde tendrils, glittering like waves of golden tinsel, tumble past her shoulders in the aftermath.

She brings the tip of the eraser to her lips, tapping it against the harsh slash of her mouth.

Once. Twice. Another time.

"Yes, we'll have to do a full rewrite. No saving you like this.

You're both too far gone. Jack put fear in his heart, too, you know."

I don't, and I should leave. Now.

"That Brady incident shouldn't have ruined you like it did. Your mate was supposed to save you, but he ran."

Ellie's last spiel upends my stealthy retreat.

"How do you know about Brady?" I ask with a stammer because that story should be locked and guarded behind the heavy metal door where I keep it—not bouncing off these bedraggled bookshelves.

She pauses, writing something with a dismissive flick of her wrist. "I know everything, girl. It's my job," she says, lifting her gaze to the ceiling. "And I would have an easier time performing my duties if someone would stop interfering with my favorite characters. No good, cold-hearted ninny."

"Right." My teeth sink into my lower lip, and I search again for Connor. Where is he? Was he murdered in the stacks?

The vibe check would match the ominous feel of this place, anyway.

"Never you mind, we'll fix you up in no time. You might glitch a few times while I get the story right. But your happily ever after is coming. I won't let Jack win this one and spoil another of my stories. If I put it somewhere cold, that should satisfy him enough to leave you alone. It may take a few days for your heart to get used to being frost free again. But you'll thank me, eventually." She pulls her cardigan tight against herself and, with a nod and pivot, glides away to some unknown destination on the heels of a pair of fuzzy socks.

Because, sure, why not add peculiar footwear to her list of oddities?

"Come along, Chia, we have matters of the heart to attend to," she hollers. A brown-spotted tabby cat jumps down from atop one of the nearby stacks, startling me with its sudden emergence.

"Holy cats!" With a tremble, I bring my clammy palm to my

chest before wiping it along the jagged edges of my mini sequin skirt. "Connor?" I croak, desperate to draw moisture to my throat. "Are you ready to go? This lady is giving me the serious creeps."

"Almost done, babe. I need one more thing. This place is great, huh? I can't believe we've never come here."

"Yeah, so weird question, but do you remember this bookstore? Because I feel like we've been to this shopping plaza a few times, and I don't remember seeing it," I ask, following the excited timbre of Connor's voice to the back of the store. A holly, jolly butt-load of winter-themed romances clutter the special recommendations shelf, assaulting my line of vision.

I roll my eyes at the manic-pixie girls with "unconventional looks" who are "not like other girls," waiting for their happily ever afters with gorgeous, brooding people undoubtedly stuffed between these abhorrent cartoon covers.

It's revolting.

And cruel. They're selling people a delusional lie, and whoever reads these sets themselves up for heartache and failure. Nothing more.

Connor barrels out of the comic book aisle, arms full of compendiums (I'm not proud I know that word), and almost bowls me over. "Sorry." He shuffles the books in his arms, trying to get a better hold of them. Two fall to the ground with a dramatic thud.

Ellie thinking this man is my soulmate is almost laughable. Nothing against Connor. He's a super sweet guy, attractive, athletic—he checks all the boxes, and I should feel the sparks for a guy like this.

But I don't.

Because true love and soulmates are just different forms of faerie tales.

Relationships are business transactions, nothing more.

Sighing, I bend down and pick up the fallen books. Zombies

litter the covers with outstretched arms as if to threaten, *we're going to eat your boyfriend's brains.*

"Terrifying," I deadpan, plopping them on Connor's pile. "This better be the only one of Jenny's loser tendencies to rub off on you. The King and Queen of Greek row titles are important to me, and the formal is too soon to be messing up now."

The last thing I need is Connor's newfound friendship with Jenny to jeopardize the social position I trucked through the previous three years to get.

Connor lops his head to the side like the golden retriever he embodies. A beautiful, blond golden with glorious dimples and sparkling azure eyes, sure. But a golden retriever nonetheless. "What's wrong with reading graphic novels?"

Graphic novels? Seriously? He knows the proper terminology?

Argh! Why the hell did Connor's English professor assign Jenny to be his tutor?

I mean, I get why he needed a tutor. But Jenny? Why couldn't our lives split off when I declared our friendship of fifteen years dead instead of this headache-inducing entanglement? This entire semester has blown because of her. Connor's gotten soft and into some bizarre stuff, like comic books and documentaries, and he even asked me if I wanted to play a tabletop game a few days ago. If he wasn't the star quarterback for Nephron University, I might be a little more worried about his status already, but if he keeps bringing me to places like this, well, I'm not immune to the side effects of Jenny-itis.

Never was.

"They're fine. Whatever." I catch the top book before it topples again. "Go check out so we can leave this hellhole. Okay?"

"You got it, babe." He leans in, pressing a kiss to my cheek before continuing an encumbered walk I dare not follow to the counter.

I'm full up on disturbed interactions for the day.

A searing pain I've grown accustomed to in the past six years stabs me in my right side, and I breathe through it, careful not to give myself away.

After my last boyfriend, Brady, couldn't handle reality, I've worked hard to hide this part of my life from Connor and my friends.

No one likes a Sad Girl™.

Pulling out my phone for a distraction, I scroll through Insta, hearting a few things I don't like, and—oh my god, no way, Taylor's new haircut looks terrible on her.

My manicured claws clack over the screen. **Love the new look, girl. Living your best life!**

Suddenly, the bell perched above the bookstore entrance chimes. My stomach flips with a groan as I glance up from my scroll-and-bitch—*you've got to be kidding me.*

It's official. This store is a special level of hell, and I'm being punished for wearing novelty socks with crocs in a former life or something. There is no other explanation for my present predicament.

## CHAPTER TWO
# Gremlins
### MADDIE

MUCH TO MY wandering eye's disappointment, Jenny Farrow appears beneath the jingling bell in her signature baseball hat, an accessory employed to hide her frizzy nest of hair. Attached at her hip like always, Mr. Thorn-in-my-Side, Seth Aarons, follows behind.

Last year, Seth caught me singing to a squirrel, and he's lorded it over my head ever since. Something about how it's a sign that I'm not as close to the "Satanic Barbie" moniker he refers to me as and that there's hope to save me yet.

He's wrong, of course. I don't need saving, especially from a spindly man desperate for a haircut and a wardrobe update. Those flannels and beanies aren't doing him any favors.

I just sometimes sing "Uptown Squirrel" to my furry friends when stressed, which shouldn't be held against me.

Since I'd rather dye my hair a putrid green than interact with either of these individuals, I whip around and pluck a book off the winter display.

"Oh my word, you're buying them all?" Jenny's voice bounces off the cracked wooden walls of the store.

"Of course I am. You made them sound amazing!" Connor replies.

Don't turn. Don't start, and they'll go away.

The light along the cream-textured page of my book recedes as a shadow crawls over my shoulder.

"I was unaware anyone in Phi Sigma Lambda Chi could read. I thought the act would rip a hole in the space-time continuum," the cold, clipped voice of Seth Aarons says behind me.

"Don't you have something better to do than be in a bookstore on a Sunday, Seth?" I sigh with a pivot and lean against the bookshelf, carefully keeping my attention on the pages in front of me. Seth isn't worth a glance.

"This may come as a shock to you, Ms. Finch, but,"—A finger latches on the top of my book, tilting my shield. "You're in a bookstore on a Sunday, too." His stern balsam fir stare bores into me, and the hideous nature that is Seth Aarons churns my stomach.

The first time I met Seth was, surprisingly—given his dour personality—at a party. Armed with an outfit curated by my influencer idol, Kennedy Spruce, I approached him—still on speaking terms with Jenny and knowing him to be her new friend. He stared with disgust at my extended hand and then opened his pinched mouth to utter one word. "No." Brushing past my shoulder, he downed a glass of punch before disappearing for good.

The whole interaction confused me for a hot minute until I learned more about him, and everything crystallized. Seth's a pretentious asshole who thinks he's better than everybody just because he's not a Swiftie or watches the latest streaming show—he's *different*.

It's grating at its best. Infuriating at its worst.

Pile that with Seth's sanctimonious BS about how I devastated Jenny when I left her, and well, let's say he's not my preferred company unless duct tape is involved.

And not in a kinky way.

Because besides his personality flaws, he's gross.

His semi-curly brown hair is way too long and scraggly under the dilapidated grey beanie he continues to sport even though it was beyond worn three winters ago, and he insists on wearing a flannel every damn day, regardless of the weather, like it'd be improper of him to expose more than his wrists to the world.

Honestly, I might die of equal parts fright and surprise if I ever saw his forearms.

"Glad to see you haven't lost that marvelous fashion sense yet." I snort, returning my eyes to the page in front of me.

"What's wrong with my flannel?" he asks, glancing down at it with a frown.

"It's a bit much, don't you think?"

"You're wearing sequins."

"Why do you insist on hovering when your company is not appreciated?" I ask with a sigh and an emphatic flip of the page. "Obsessed much?"

"No, sorry, Finch. For whatever reason, Wednesday Addams and Elle Woods's love child isn't my type." He slides his hands into the pockets of his worn denim.

"And yet you continue to hover."

"You're in my section." He tugs the top of a spine, pulling it out of its cramped spot and pages through its contents.

"This is the romance section."

"And?" He doesn't glance up, and it irks me to no end. Talking to me is a privilege he shouldn't take for granted.

"Shouldn't you be reading like, I don't know, sci-fi or military fiction or something?"

"Well, that's an awful patriarchal view on romance there, Ms. Finch. Guys enjoy stories where people fall in love, too. Plus, they're kind of like manuals for certain things." He continues and raises his eyes to meet mine, wearing his signature crooked grin. A facial expression that's almost as infuriating as the man himself. "I'd be more than happy to recommend a few to Connor if it'd help take the edge off whatever this is." He gestures at me, returning to his book.

"Edge?" I squeak out. For whatever reason, this discussion is forcing an unwelcome heat on my cheeks. Hopefully, whatever he's reading will hold his attention long enough for them to chill.

"That's one way he could do it, sure. You're not a subtle blusher, are you, Satanic Barbie?" he asks before humming a far too familiar Billy Joel song.

"Lumberjack Frasier," I mutter under my breath.

"Darth Blair Waldorf."

"I'm shocked you know anything about Gossip Girl, Tragically More-Annoying Ross Geller. I assumed your television knowledge was reserved for CNN documentaries or something."

"I'm full of surprises, Madeline." He picks his gaze up, meeting mine for a fraction, before dropping to my lips like he's waiting for my response.

"God, you're obsessed with me."

"Contrary to popular belief, you're not everyone's type," he deadpans, but a decidedly pink tinge to his cheeks gives him away. He's not as cool as he's trying to play it.

"And you're not Jenny's." His book snaps shut. *Got him.* I flash him a saccharine smile. "But maybe those cute puppy-dog eyes you flash her way will wear her down soon enough. Who knows?" I boop his nose with the condescending giggle I've mastered over the years and pivot away with a hair flip... oof... right into Connor's broad chest.

Connor's hands fall to my hips, stabilizing me. "Hey, babe, Jenny's going to show me some graphic novels she thinks I might like, and then we can go. Sound good?"

My ex-best friend, Jenny, hovers behind Connor's shoulder. I meet her eyes, shaded under the brim of her hat, and find the hurt hanging in her chocolate brown irises, no less faded after three years. A pang of remorse tugs on my conscience, and I bury it.

Betraying her was the cost I paid for my new life. I was initially reluctant, a large part of me desperate to cling to her as if she was a part of my soul rather than another person. But three years later, with the quarterback of the football team and multiple other guys wrapped around my finger, a sorority house full of people looking up to me, and a thriving social life on campus, I can say that sacrifice was worth it.

Even if I carry the guilt of my actions around.

"No, Connor," I whine. "I want to leave. Now."

His infectious smile curls down. "It'll just be a sec—promise," he says, leaning in and kissing my cheek.

Okay, but why bother asking if it was okay if my answer didn't matter?

A book drops behind me to a muffled. "Shit."

Connor glances over my shoulder, and a crease forms between his brows. "Hey, aren't you—"

"Jenny's friend, yeah." Seth cuts him off with a panicked edge to his voice. I face him, curious about what has him so flustered, but he's just standing there, pink-cheeked, trying to restock a few fallen books.

"No, I mean sure—you probably are." Connor scratches his head. "But didn't I play football against you a few years ago, bro?"

"As in, Seth was a collegiate athlete? No way," I laugh.

"Actually, he—" Jenny starts.

"Has some books to recommend to Madeline," Seth cuts in. "So why don't you show Connor those graphic novels, Jenny?"

"Right..." Jenny's eyebrow furrows, glancing at me, but she shakes her head and retreats. At least she's had the decency to leave me alone during this unfortunate episode.

Crossing my arms in front of my chest, I pivot back to Seth, observing the quick bob of his throat and shaking hands. "Why were you just weirder than normal?"

"Was I?" The tips of Seth's ears burn a crimson red, and he tugs his beanie down over them.

"Not that I care, but yeah. You were. You still are."

"Forced proximity to you is hazardous to my health." He shrugs.

I drop my eyes to his footwear. Doc Martens. Of course. The damage my heel could cause ground into his toes would be minimal, but the act itself would be satisfying enough.

A soft laugh from the back of the stacks wafts its way to us. Or I could stomp on someone with flimsier footwear.

My head snaps towards the laughter to find Jenny against the wall, Connor's forearm resting above her head. He reaches out and touches her arm, and that's it. Something breaks inside of me. While I've operated under a don't touch Jenny-Code for three years, this is too far. I can't deal with these two anymore.

With my fists clenched at my side, I storm towards the happy couple.

"Hey there, tiger. Remember your code." Seth catches my hand, whipping me into another aisle of romance books.

Sparks fly from his contact, shooting up my arm, like even my body's repulsed by him. I chase the terrible sensation away with a shake. "What code?" I ask since it's not supposed to be public information.

The lights flicker around us and the stereo playing *The Christmas Waltz* glitches, spiraling the same lyrics about Christmas being a time for falling in love, over and over and over.

Seth's forest green eyes narrow, pinning a stony stare on me. Gold flecks rimming his iris twinkle like a bough of pine wrapped with sparkling white lights.

"It's been three years, and you've never sunken your manicured claws into Jenny, Pookie. I'm not dumb. Either you know nothing you could do to hurt her more than you already have, or even the Ice Queen has limits."

For the first time in forever, Jenny's nickname for me punctures my heart, like somehow Seth cracked and shattered everything I'd worked so hard to build up with one six-letter word.

I bury the guilt threatening to bubble to the surface, but the box I've kept it locked up in is too small to fit the growing deluge.

"Maybe it's time to try something new," I force, nowhere near as confident as usual. I take a step, hoping Seth overlooks the waver in my voice. He blocks my path. "Seth Aarons, I swear, I'm not afraid to claw your eyes out if you don't move." I go to push him, and he catches my wrists. My back hits the shelves with force as he pins me against the stack.

Dust explodes off the shelf, and the sweet scent of freshly baked sugar cookies overwhelms my airways. This whole thing is a terrible dream. It has to be.

Warmth curls around me as Seth and my chests press together. My respiration system fails.

"Seth, I'm flattered, but I'm awfully taken." I bat my eyelashes at him, hoping everything comes out laced with the mockery I intend but can't seem to supply.

"Retract the claws, and I'll let go," he whispers harshly, inches from my lips.

My stomach churns with his proximity and ties itself into a knot.

Another drag of air. Another heaving breath. "Consider them withdrawn."

"That's a good girl." He winks. An odd sensation sparks alive between my thighs at his response. I cough in my recovery.

With widened eyes, he steps back on his heel, rubbing the back of his head.

Light streams in over the bookcase. A halo forms around him. His sharp angles and dimpled chin pop under the natural spotlight.

His tongue darts out to moisten his lips, and I'm suddenly mesmerized. My fingers trace the seam of my lips before I can register what I'm doing. In haste, I rip my hand to my side, rapping it against the bookshelf behind me.

"Ow, fuck." I shake out the stinging pain. Maybe that'll teach my damn hand a lesson about going rogue.

Seth whips around on impact, almost like he's the one who slapped the shelf. "You okay?" He asks softly, cocking his head to the side.

"Fine. Sorry."

The pink of his lips curves into a crooked smirk that makes my heart do weird fluttering things. It's official. Seth Aarons's aura is suffocating me. Death is imminent. "Yeah, now I know you're not okay. I didn't know you knew that word, Ms. Finch." He grips my hand, rubbing the point of contact.

"Neither did I," I say, mouth slightly agape.

A gentle breeze swirls around us. A pull tightens in my gut like it's tugging me towards Seth, and I almost don't want to fight it. Complacency feels natural.

Asphyxiation causes hallucinations, right?

He flashes an almost affectionate smile as his soft gaze glows like warm candlelight over my face. His thumb massages my palm, turning my hand over and inspecting it. "You sure you're okay?"

"Mmhmm." Sparks follow in the wake of his touch, and goosebumps pebble the flesh on my arms.

An overhead light flickers, and when my eyes adjust, every feeling is as it should be.

"Seth Aarons," I hiss. "Get your greasy paws off my hands."

He blinks. Once. Twice. Withdrawing his hand, he shakes his head like he's trying to snap himself out of something. "Right. Sorry, I—thought your hand might be broken."

"What the hell?" Connor's angry voice cuts through all our confusion as he thunders in from the top of the aisle.

Seth straightens with a few more rapid blinks, pulling a book out beside my head. Shivers race down my spine as his heat draws closer.

"This should help with your problem, Barbie." The bastard winks at me, shoving a book with a shirtless postal worker on the cover titled *Male Delivery: Over-Sized Package* in my hand and attempting to walk past Connor.

With his fists balled to his side, my boyfriend's broad figure mirrors and blocks Seth's steps. While Lumberjack Frasier's tall, gangly frame looms over Connor, Connor has the muscle. Although I would love for Seth to get his ass kicked, there's this odd part clawing its way to the surface that wants to protect him at all costs, and I blame this fucking store.

"Connor, he's fine. Leave him," I snap.

His gaze oscillates between Seth and me. "But he was—you were—"

"He wasn't doing anything. Seriously, do you think I would let a loser like that touch me without losing his testicles?"

"But I saw him."

"Baby, you saw nothing." I shake my head, getting closer and pressing my body against his. That I have to do any of this, given that Connor and Jenny were in a very similar position only two minutes ago, is complete BS, but I'll fight about double standards with Connor another time. Right now, I want to leave this GD store, and placating Connor's ego is the best strategy to expedite that.

I give him three seconds before he scoops me up and lays the thickest, sloppiest kiss on my lips to mark his territory.

One. Two—

On three, without fail, Connor's face eats mine.

It's wet and unpleasant, much like the word "moist" itself.

"It's a kiss. You're not supposed to drown her," Seth says dryly as he walks past us.

Seriously, Seth? I'm saving your ass right now.

Connor pulls away from my lips, shooting daggers in Seth's direction, and I draw him back down, moaning in his mouth.

"Jenny, you good? We gotta pick up the toys before going to the Youth Center; they should be ready now," Seth hollers while the lights flicker above.

"Right! Bye, Madeline," Jenny says as she skirts by us.

Madeline. Not Maddie or Pookie. Madeline. She's finally accepted who I am now.

Good.

"Bye, Pixie!" The words fly past my ultra-fine, five-layered filter system and into the world, falling in a shocked hush.

What the hell was that?

Three years. Not once have I slipped up and used my nickname for Jenny.

So why did I do that?

The bell perched over the door rings, signaling the Torture Twin's departure, and I breathe lighter. I can figure out why the old Maddie keeps crawling her flat-belly way to the surface like a worm avoiding a deluge later.

Slowly, Connor's gaze travels south of my lips. "You're so sexy. You know that?" He trails a finger along my collarbone, and the shivers and sparks that followed Seth's touch are absent.

Flannel *is* a great conductor of static electricity, though.

That would explain it.

"Hey, for real, Connor. Please go check out."

"Right, I'm just waiting for the checkout lady. I don't know where she went."

"Almost there." Ellie's shrill voice punctures my earlobes as she claps her hands in a rush from the backroom. "It takes me a few days, of course. I hope that's okay. I need to plot. All about those beats, you know; no good comes from pantsing these things; that's how you get chapters that ramble and only happen in one location. Those kinds of chapters need to end! But you got a taste with him, I'm sure. Do you see, girl? Do you see what you could feel?" she asks, scanning Connor's stack of graphic novels piled on the counter.

A taste of what? That odd sense of vulnerability that washed over me with Seth?

Thinking about his lips far too much?

Is that what she means?

Seriously, what witchcraft and/or drugs does she have back there?

Connor glances around the store before leaning into me. "Who is she talking to?" he whispers.

Me. And I wouldn't say I like it.

"No idea. But please, can we go? Now," I whine.

He nods, grabbing a comically—pun intended and regretted —large bag from Ellie, whose eyes are trained, lifeless, beyond both our shoulders. "That's it. That's your wound. Of course, it is," she says in a trance. The faulty lights flicker and cast her face in harsh shadows. Something tightens its grip around my chest, squeezing it far too tight. "And I know just the lesson!" Ellie raises an emphatic finger to the sky. The lighting stabilizes.

I rub a palm over my heart, attempting to release the gathering tension and wipe away the phantom feeling of Seth's fingers brushing against my heart line.

"Bye?" Connor tilts his head, starting a backward retreat as I race to the door, busting through to the humid Texas air and freedom.

I am never going to a bookstore again.

## CHAPTER THREE

SETH

I. AM. Fucked.

Three years ago, I snuffed out that damn flame that ignited the first moment I saw Madeline standing in the kitchen she shared with Jenny, bleary-eyed, tear-stained cheeks, and still somehow a god-damn vision. It took what? Two seconds of forced proximity, a potent dose of her intoxicating rosewater scent, and boom—re-ignition, combustion, death.

Madeline Finch is not the type of person you fall in love with unless you hate yourself, and since I've developed a healthy dose of self-esteem over the past few years, I'm not interested in opening that box of doom. Luckily, whatever sparking fire was about to burn for her was thoroughly suffocated when that rabid creature almost clawed Jenny's eyes out.

Er, well, mostly.

Today, the flame's a bit more stubborn.

Walking away from the bookstore with Jenny, I rub a hand over my chest, evening my breaths and studying the cracks on the sidewalk. Smoke rises from the charred post oak pits at the BBQ restaurant across the street, carrying a familiar comfort through my lungs. The usual cravings and hunger pangs accompanying the thoughts of brisket and ribs never materialize. I don't have the appetite for anything since a peculiar ache buried itself in my abdomen while I was in the stacks with Maddie.

Nausea over the idea of almost kissing her, no doubt.

"Did you hear it?" Jenny glances at me; a pleading, questioning gaze passes through her piercing amber eyes. Warm and welcoming, unlike the glacial frost in Madeline's blue ones. "She said 'Pixie,' right? Like, she said it back for once!" Since we left the bookstore, she's been analyzing our little run-in with Store Brand-Regina George. I could tell her what almost happened, that if I hadn't sacrificed myself, she would have found herself unable to see, but Jenny doesn't want the truth. And I can't be the person to break her heart more than Madeline already has.

She wants what we all want during the holidays. She wants hope.

"Maddie was definitely softer," Jenny mutters to herself.

In the three years I've known Jenny, she's been like this—hopeful and far too forgiving. She wants her best friend back, and Madeline saying "Pixie" is going to be her green fucking light, beckoning her across a vast expanse of bleak, troubled waters.

Jenny had called Madeline by her full name for the first time in passing, too, like she had finally accepted that her friend no longer existed.

Fuck.

Madeline doesn't deserve this kind of loyalty, much like Jenny did nothing to deserve someone betraying her the way Satanic Barbie did. How anyone could wake up one day and decide they don't want to be friends with Jenny is beyond me. She's perfect. From her humor to her brilliant mind, her obsession with fantasy and graphic novels, or the smaller things like the crease that sits atop her adorable button nose when she's puzzling something out.

"Hey." The gold lights wrapped around the base of passing palm trees reflect in the wistful gaze she flashes in my direction. "Did you feel something in the bookstore?"

Like the world was glitching for a brief second, and I suddenly knew the power of taming a wild beast?

"You mean more than the hefty dose of evil wrapping its icy talons around us?" I ask.

Jenny giggles, an act always accompanied by her one winking dimple and a snort. My heart flutters at the endearing nature of it all. "No. Well, maybe more like the absence of the talons?" She shakes her head. "Never mind, you'd just make fun of me."

"Well, now I have to know." I grin. Jenny's full of these wild theories pinned around a powerful belief in the unbelievable. As in, she's a twenty-one-year-old who still believes in Santa Claus and fae, and she'd sell her soul for some fictional man named Rhysand she's determined exists in an alternate realm.

"Okay." She worries her teeth across her bottom lip, and I fight back the odd confident voice that's been vying for dominance inside me since the incident with Madeline in the stacks. Currently, it's whispering, *darling, let me kiss that worry right off.* "But no teasing!" She wags an accusatory finger in my face.

"I would never." I raise my hands in surrender as the timid part of me reasserts himself.

I'll confess that I'm in love with her another time, then.

"Liar." She peeks at me beneath the maroon brim of her baseball hat, the word *fireheart* embroidered across the panels. "Do you remember when I ran up to you that first day of chemistry class asking if you wanted to be study buddies?"

God, do I. I was such a down-in-the-dumps dope on my first day of transferring to Ephron University, so unsure of who the fuck I was anymore. The only thing I was sure of was that I was no longer the douche I had been for most of high school and my first year of college.

It's easy to be a douche-canoe. Especially when you're a five-star quarterback recruit at one of the top football-playing universities in the country, equipped with a full scholarship, and talk swirling around the media about you being a first-round draft pick when you decide to go pro. Throw in Heisman contention your first year and a gorgeous girlfriend of five years with a modeling contract and a doting Instagram following, and you've got the perfect recipe for a self-assured asshole that deserves to be hit by a truck.

Which is precisely what happened. When in a stupid, freak moment, right before our bowl game, I crossed the damn street with my eyes glued to my phone and my girlfriend's recent bikini-clad Instagram post, and a truck-driver shifted his eyes off the road to pick another playlist and truck met body. My body met hell and months and months of physical therapy.

And I met reality without football.

My girlfriend, Kennedy, left me the second it became apparent my identity as a college quarterback was slipping away, and my friends on the team ghosted me pretty damn quick, too.

I couldn't handle the pity on campus or the tuition without the scholarship. I transferred to one of the state schools the following year, determined to keep a low profile since my story had permeated the national media.

Jenny was the first person I met on campus. She barreled her way into my life with a massive smile in our shared Chemistry 101 class. I was reluctant to let anyone close, but as we worked together in labs and I learned more about her, letting her into my life wasn't an option. She just was.

"Don't take this the wrong way because I'm happy we're friends and everything, but I attacked you with enthusiasm that day because of your aura. It matches Maddie's." Her nose twitches. "Well, it did anyway."

"What do you mean my aura matched Maddie's?" I smirk, crossing my arms and leaning against the warm glass of the toy store's display window, where I'm sure the model train running along the edge of the window now looks like it's entering my ass. Jenny's theories are one of my favorite sources of entertainment.

"You two were soulmates, I think."

"Wow, insult me more, Farrow."

"I don't mean now!" She tosses her hands in the air. "I don't know, everyone has this halo around them, and that first year, yours and Maddie's matched before hers flickered out."

"And what happened to mine?" I shield my eyes as the afternoon sun bears down on us. Beads of sweat form on my temple, and I regret the ink on my forearm that's an ode to my former life, more so than usual. I should have moved to Alaska after everything. It'd be so much easier to keep it covered.

"It's receded a bit. I mean, it's still there, but it's like it's dormant. I don't know. Sometimes I see it flare when she's around, but not peacefully. It's like it's screaming in pain."

"That would explain the terrible stomachache she always elicits."

"It would, actually," she says, pinching her lips between her index finger and thumb. "But today, it was like hers was malfunctioning, and there was a moment where you two were in sync again. You didn't feel it?"

My mind flashes back to the stacks and the sudden relentless tug to crash my lips onto Madeline's and make her forget her name, even though I know better. Even though, as she said, she's very taken.

I didn't care.

For a second, all I could think about was how—I didn't even want her to be mine. No, I skipped that step, and she just was.

Mine.

My hand to take care of. My person to kiss.

"Nah." I shake my head. I need to get a grip. Jenny's bizarre theories are adorable and harmless as long as I don't buy into them, especially this one. "You had to be seeing stuff again."

Jenny places her hands on her hips, raising a challenging brow at me. "Okay, now I know you felt something."

"No way. I was saving your ass. That's all." I pick my lean up off the storefront and nudge her. "But seriously, Jenny. Whatever is going on with you and Connor, please quit it. I'd rather not be in close quarters with the Wicked Bitch of the West again."

And notice me. Please.

Her cheeks flush, and she mutters something under her breath.

"I'm sorry. What was that?"

"But he's my person. We match." She scuffs her shoe along the concrete pavement.

My heart sinks. Connor's everything I used to be, so to hear Jenny say shit like that, well, it fucking hurts. Because Jenny Farrow deserves the type of guy who would worship the ground she walks on.

Like me. Now.

The man who's been dying to get out of the friend zone for years because I know everything that makes Jenny amazing.

Like her kindness and her drive to help others.

And how she can't eat a piece of pizza without covering her face in the sauce. Every. Damn. Time.

Or how she's the grump to my sunshine before coffee, but the minute that caffeine drip hits, she becomes the most radiant star in the solar system.

"No offense, Jenny, because I appreciate how you love all this fantasy stuff, but maybe it's time to bury that aura thing. People like Madeline and Connor were made for each other, not us." I open the front door of the toy store, Bailey's Toy Chest, trying to hide my frown. Respectfully, the friend zone sucks ass sometimes. "Why don't we get the toys?"

Inside, we're accosted by upbeat Christmas music, bits of wrapping paper spewed across the store, an Elf on the Shelf creepily watching us, and way too many grumpy adults trying to find something the store doesn't have.

I glance around, attempting to locate the store owner, Mr. Bailey, in the chaos. His eyes connect with mine, hovering by a display of stuffed animals, and he holds up his finger as if to say, "one minute."

Suddenly, a dog hand puppet pops into my line of vision. "Believe in the aura, Seth. The aura is real," it says in a mangled British accent. "Madeline Finch was your soulmate."

"I thought we were dropping this," I say, nuzzling the dog away from my face. "And your accent is terrible, by the way."

Jenny punctures my heart with her innocent doe-eyes. "First off, ouch. Second off, what? I am. But Sir Woofington Wagglebottoms the third here, well, he's a hopeless romantic."

"Sir Woofington Wagglebottoms?"

"The third."

"That's a ruff name, poor guy."

Sir Woofington Wagglebottoms... the third... covers his eyes with his paws. "So was that pun, but my Maddie would have loved it."

"I hate to tell you this, *Pixie*, but your Maddie is dead. It's Madeline now."

"Okay, so let's say I give up on the Maddie thing with you; I still think it's time we talk about you putting yourself out there again, bucko. It's been three years, and you're a good-looking fellow. Maybe you should ask someone to the Winter Formal. I scored us both invitations, you know." She walks towards the puppet rack to put Sir Woofington in his appropriate spot before her grabby fingers find a wooden snake to bend and twist. I nervously fidget while she's a safe distance away.

Maybe I could tell Jenny how I feel. While I don't love the idea of risking the only friendship I have in my post-football era, there's something—I don't know if it's the jealousy of seeing her with Connor or the frustration of that run-in with Madeline, but I want to shout in this toy store, *I love you, I love you, I love you.* And she did just say I was a good-looking fellow, so I have that going for me too.

"Yeah, so, Jenny, about that." I rub my neck and shift my beanie. She pulls back a tiny metal bus. It zooms across its display and crashes into a Lincoln Log cabin that doesn't survive the collision. Jenny's eyes widen, sidestepping away from the crime scene. Marching towards the display, I fix it up before returning to the counter to the sound of multiple boxes crashing. "Get over here," I whisper. "I'm trying to tell you something, and there are children in here minding their hands better than you are right now."

"Oh! Hey! Did you get the romance book you wanted?"

"No—and that's not—" I sigh, pinching the bridge of my nose. This is why I've never told Jenny how I feel, because every time I work up the nerve, she becomes chaos incarnate. "Satanic Barbie got in the way. I'll go back in a few days. Not a big deal."

Romance novels became my saving grace as I was recovering from knee surgery and the other injuries I suffered. It started because it was the only thing within reach at my mom's house when she went out to run an errand, but the guarantee of a happily ever after hooked me. I needed it after my disastrous ending with Kennedy, her engagement ring still burning a hole in my sock drawer upstairs.

"What I wanted to say to you, Jenny, was, well, I'm wondering —would you maybe want to go to the formal with me?"

"Like as friends?" she asks, yanking something out of the bin of small toys meant for stocking stuffers. The store lights flicker again to curses of the failing Texas power grid, and Jenny meets the worried look I can't control with a frown. "Oh, Seth," she whispers. "That's not what you mean, is it?"

I shake my head, the tone of that follow-up question telling me everything I need to know.

"Aww, that's so cute, and I'm flattered. But—" She twists her hands and grimaces. "Oh, this is awkward." My stomach churns at the fake tone lacing her every word. It's a condescending tone that Kennedy perfected, and I've heard out of Madeline's mouth many times, but never Jenny's. She's too genuine to use a tone like that. "Connor's going to break up with Maddie soon, and I'm planning to go to the formal with him."

"You're going to let him do that to your Pookie?" I ask. Images of Madeline forlorn on a bench and dateless for the formal tug on my heartstrings. It shouldn't bother me; she deserves it, but for some inexplicable reason, I can't stomach it.

Jenny sighs, not meeting my eyes.

"I mean, it's not like she wouldn't do the same thing to me."

"But Jenny, you're not Madeline—that's the difference."

"True, but I don't know. Connor said something in the bookstore, and I've been thinking about it on our walk, and maybe it's time to do something for myself. Let Maddie be the one to know what it's like to be left behind for a change." Finally, she returns my stare, but the lack of warmth in her eyes sucks the air out of my lungs. "Anyway, I hope this doesn't make anything awkward between us, Seth, because our friendship is important to me, and—"

"Consider everything status quo." I offer, searching for the comfort that's held me for all these years.

But the icy reflection that greets me belongs to someone else.

"Oh, good. Get the toys for me, and I'll get us some drinks from Cup of Jo's. Your treat?" she says with a giggle, booping my nose.

I dip my head and nod, pulling out my credit card and hoping there will be sufficient funds for her. "Get yourself something. I'm fine."

"Thanks! You're the best!" She tosses her arms around me, wrapping me up in a big hug, and I return the gesture half-heartedly. The nervous flutters I've grown accustomed to when we touch mix with a pang of dread and remorse.

Yeah, definitely fucked.

## CHAPTER FOUR
## *Scrooged*
### MADDIE

**ON THE FIFTH** day of weirdness, Seth Aarons gave to me ten ignored text messages, five missed phone calls, two almost run-ins, and a visit under a live oak tree.

I had avoided him at all costs. Whatever stomachache he elicited in that bookstore was unpleasant at best and hazardous at worst.

I need to focus on what's important. There's still some last-minute planning for the Phi Sigma Lambda Chi Annual Winter Formal to check off, which now includes buying an extra generator, just in case the ever-present flickering lights give out. Damn Texas grid. And I need to write my acceptance speech for when I'm awarded the crown as Queen of Greek Row. A title I've worked tirelessly to get.

Thanking my asshole of an ex-boyfriend, Brady, for my current success will be at the top of my spiteful speech since his words got my ass in gear to achieve all this. *Look, you're cute and all, Maddie, but you're not worth the hassle.*

It frustrated me, sure, when Ellie brought him up a few days ago at the bookstore, opening a door I'd much rather keep barred shut. But after tomorrow, there won't be a door to guard anymore, and I can send it through the wood chipper for the ending it deserves.

Three years ago, when Brady dumped me, I thought his parting words would break me. My doting parents had referred to me as a burden my entire life, so when he reaffirmed my worth, I just... broke. But a week after our break-up, in a milkshake haze at the diner with Jenny, Brady Grey, and his new girlfriend, soon-to-be Queen of Greek Row, Lacey Cane had one more life lesson to pass along.

Where Brady walked with me with his arm slung around my shoulder in a possessive manner, he followed Lacey two steps behind like an obedient puppy. Anything she barked for, he provided. Nothing was too much of a hassle then.

Why?

Because Lacey was worth something with her flawless appearance and social status.

And if I ever wanted to be worth the hassle, I'd have to invest in those things too.

Unfortunately, I needed to cut something out of my life.

Someone whom I loved more than life itself.

And was blowing bubbles into her milkshake.

Jenny had to go. She was quirky, awkward, and ignorant about the things that mattered, and I couldn't afford to drag any deadweight along with me for my climb to the top.

I don't care if Seth thinks it was cruel. Sometimes we must lose to gain.

And now I'm a day away from achieving everything I've worked so hard for.

Sighing away my trip down memory lane, I grab my phone and silence the ringer before turning up the music I'm blaring to drown out the sound of Abby's Christmas music downstairs. How many times does this woman have to listen to Mariah Carey's *All I Want for Christmas is You?*

The beginning jingles reset, permeating my wall of Harry Styles, and apparently, the limit doesn't exist for Abby this year.

Whoever Mariah is asking for, dear Santa, can you please, for the love of all that is holly, give it to her this year? I've had my fill of that song in this house.

Dropping onto my bed, I grab my heating pad and place it on my abdomen to quiet the pain roaring there.

I thought about letting the girls know about my endometriosis a few times. But after overhearing one of my sisters last year say that she thought people with chronic illnesses are sad, I decided it was best that the only person left on campus who knew was Jenny—who would never dream of breaking my confidence on the matter. She's too good.

It's not a simple thing to hide, but it is doable, so I push through every day, ensuring my exterior reflects the perfection I strive for, even when my interior is a dumpster fire. Relaxing with my favorite baking show playing on my laptop and laying back like this is the only time I let myself give in and acknowledge the pain.

If anyone saw me, they'd have a field day with my unkempt appearance, but this is my favorite part of the day—Madeline time. My hair's twisted up in a topknot with a spa headband to push back my bangs, and I plastered a swamp green mask on my face. To complete the cozy AF aesthetic, I'm wrapped in an old baggy shirt from my "Maddie" days. It's a shirt Jenny bought me because she thought it was hilarious, and I guess it is. It says "Nar Wars" in big yellow letters and has two narwhals with lightsabers instead of horns. I hardly ever wear it, but something today tugged at me to snuggle with it.

So I did.

There isn't anyone here, so what's the harm?

Two hard raps on my door force me to pause my baking video with a loud sigh. Everyone in the house knows I need this me time and they've always either respected or feared me enough to comply.

"Enter," I say, not bothering to hide my irritation.

Haley, a pledge who has yet to learn proper fear, peeks her

annoyingly flawless little First-Year head in. The Christmas music and my frustration with this intrusion grow louder without the hard-oak barrier.

"Madeline, a guy named Seth is here to see you." Her eyes widen when she takes in the green mush on my face. "He's kind of cute. Want me to send him in?"

"No," I hiss.

"Cali said you'd want to see him. I just—"

"Seth, go right in." The smooth, plotting tone of Cali Grant grates harder against my eardrums than Mariah's wails. Cali has been after my spot atop the PSL Chi house for so long that I'm not surprised she's trying this right now. "Let him in, Haley."

"No, Haley, don't!" I panic.

"I'm so sorry, but she scares me," Haley whispers.

"I should scare you," I say through gritted teeth. But it's too late. I've been so in my head the past few days about my weird interaction at the bookstore with that store clerk and calling Jenny "Pixie" that I haven't put enough energy into keeping my edges sharp, and now Seth Aarons is about to enter my bedroom,

Are you happy neurotic Maddie?

Madeline.

Fuck. Focus.

My face is green. My hair is gross. I'm wearing a punny, nerd shirt, and it's too late to correct any of this.

New strategy. Pretend like none of this is a big deal. If I don't act like I'm embarrassed, maybe Seth won't pick up on how humiliating this is.

I return my gaze to my computer, lying on my stomach to conceal my heating pad and narwhals, and cross my legs, letting them flick high in the air. My insides come alive, like a grand opening of an amusement park with its flips, churns, and sugary sweet anticipation.

Again, a peculiar, nostalgic sensation fights for real estate of my mind and body, like all the control I've mastered over the years to keep the dorky First-Year repressed is unraveling.

"Hey." I nod as he bows under the door frame. "What's up?"

Seth shuts the door and freezes when his eyes fall on me. His lips pull into a slow, devastating smile as his eyebrows creep upward. Whether in confusion or surprise, I can't tell.

Without a word of acknowledgment, his hand slides into his pocket and retrieves his phone.

Shit, does he seriously think he's going to take a picture? Oh, hell no.

But he's a fast draw, and before I know it, a white flash assaults my eyes while I'm lunging toward his phone. An internal pain screeches with the sudden motion, but I do my best to ignore it.

Seth raises his phone above his head, and while I'm not small at five-eleven, I forgot how much taller he is than me. He must be at least six-four. Maybe even six-five, the way he loomed over Connor's six-two frame.

"Come on, Peter Stalker. No loser paparazzi in the bedroom." I jump up, trying to reach for it. Seth angles the phone down, and it flashes again. "Do you have a death wish, Aarons? If you don't quit it and delete those right now, I swear, I'll kick you so hard, it'll make your ancestors' balls recede too."

Seth chuckles, scrolling through his photos above my head, his other hand placed over his sensitive area. "Come on. You look cute." He continues scrolling. Maybe I could bite him. I doubt my teeth would penetrate his flannel barrier enough to cause significant damage, but it's worth trying.

"Cute is what—" I lunge and miss. "Guys call girls when they have nothing nice to say but don't want to come off like an ass." I reach my grabby hands, brushing the bottom of his phone with my fingertips. Damn.

"Really? Because cute is what I say when something is cute, and I want to call it cute."

"Cute is for the average, Aarons," I huff. "And I'm not average."

"Well, obviously." He rolls his eyes. "Oh. This is definitely the one." He angles the photo at me and smiles. "Madeline Grinch."

"Har. Har." With a bounce on my toes, I swipe for the phone again but land awkwardly on Seth's aggravating feet instead. His free arm wraps around my back to stabilize me, and those damn electric shocks I felt at the bookstore follow. My breath hitches at the sparking sensation that terrorizes my nervous system. Seth's stare dances over my lips, and the evergreen wildwood held within gives way to a mischievous glint.

The pull to rise on my toes for a far more disconcerting reason heightens, and I swallow it back down. "Seth. Come on. You came into my safe space. That's not fair," I pout. I hate the damsel in distress card, but with Seth's savior complex, it's a strategy I'm willing to employ.

Desperate measures and all that.

"This wouldn't have been an issue if you had responded to my calls or texts over the past five days."

Or maybe Seth is that big of an asshat. Back to attack mode, then.

Seth lets his guard down, and I dive forward in a last-ditch effort. He shifts out of the way, and I come close to crashing into the wall.

"You're going to hurt yourself," he says flatly.

"Well then, maybe you should delete them. We wouldn't want this poor, cute little girl to get hurt, would we?"

He peers at me beneath his thick lashes and snorts. "Tell you what, have this talk with me, and I'll delete them, okay?"

"You are a manipulative, demonic thorn in my side, Aarons," I mutter.

"Just returning the favor, Madeline," he says curtly.

My shoulders sag in defeat, and I trudge to the en-suite bathroom in my room. "Let me go wash this off."

Collecting myself at the sink, I take a deep breath and repeat; *you are still worth something*. With no eyebrows filled in, or contour on my face, it's like I'm going into battle without armor, meagerly equipped with a pair of false lashes I didn't bother to remove earlier and minimal training at approaching anyone fresh-faced.

My hands shake. I haven't let anyone see me like this since Brady made it abundantly clear that my vulnerability was a flaw to smooth away.

*Not the time to think about it,* I chide before turning the knob to my bedroom, barely ready for a fight.

Seth is sitting on my bed, eyes sparkling with amusement when he takes me in.

"Don't laugh." I glare at him.

He sticks his palms up in the air. "I wasn't going to laugh. Can we talk about this shirt, though?"

I was hoping he wouldn't notice.

"No. Unless you came over here to talk about my at-home leisurewear."

"Not originally, but now that I've seen this, I'd love to devote some time to the conversation before I go out and buy one for myself." He crosses one of his long, lean legs over his opposite knee like we're best friends at a sleepover about to share some hot gos.

"Oh. No bother, you can have this one," I say, gripping the worn, cotton hem of my t-shirt and raising it over my head. There's no way Seth can handle a woman in a sports bra with the same undeserved bravado he entered this conversation with, and I run without a t-shirt all the time.

"No. It's fine." Seth stands brusquely. His hands clutch mine, and he halts my disrobing. My pulse skitters along my heart line when his thumb meets the inside of my wrist. I swallow, looking up at him. I'd never admit this to anyone, but I don't think the sparking sensation is a byproduct of his flannels anymore.

His eyes dance over my face, then still, gazing at me with a blazing intensity that threatens to incinerate the multiple barriers raised to protect my heart and soul. "I like seeing you without your mask on, Ms. Finch," he murmurs. His right dimple winks as he flashes me a lopsided grin.

And I'm reduced to nothing but warm, sputtering embers and wind-blown ashes.

Voices clamor with heavy footsteps along the top of the stairs, nearing my room. "Yeah, she's right inside—" The knob rattles, and the swoosh of the door swinging open follows.

With my back to the door, I have no clue who's coming in, but by the way Seth's shoulders raise as the rest of his body goes rigid, it can't be good.

"Hands," I whisper. At the same time, a familiar voice grunts, "What the hell?"

Connor.

In a panic, Seth whisks his hands behind his back.

I whip around, only to catch my boyfriend's backside marching back out of the room. "Connor, I can explain."

"No need. We're done, Madeline." He doesn't glance again in my direction before he slams the door shut, and footsteps thunder down the stairs.

I lunge towards the door with a harried "shit."

"Hold on, Madeline—there's something I need to tell you." Seth's fingers brush against the loose hanging cotton of my sleeve, reaching for me.

I shrug his fingers off. "Not now, Seth." I huff. With one day left before the formal, I can't have shit like this exploding in my life. Whatever Seth came over to say will have to wait. I bolt out my bedroom door and sprint down the stairs. It's impressive, given my speed, that I don't tumble down them instead.

"Oh, did you not want him to see you with Seth?" Cali's voice follows me.

"Suck a dick, Cali," I call back.

"Did you hear what she just said to her sister? That's not PSL Chi behavior," Cali's whispers accompany me as I run out the door barefoot. With my hair a mess, a huge nerdy t-shirt on, and booty shorts, none of what I'm doing is the dignified PSL Chi way, and I will pay for it later. But if I get Connor back, I'll have a fighting chance.

Connor's figure trudges further ahead, illuminated under the harsh light of a nearby streetlamp as he marches away from Greek Row. I fly over dying grass, piercing my feet like shards of glass in the cool night air. Apparently, a cold front came in. Good ol' Texas. It can be summer in the morning and winter by five.

"Connor, wait."

"Go back to Seth, Madeline," he tosses over his shoulder. "There's nothing to talk about."

"It's not what you think."

"No more lying. I'm not that stupid, and Jenny told me what was happening between you two. Said you've been sneaking around behind my back for weeks."

Wait, Jenny said what?

My Pookie would never, even if I deserved it.

"She's the one who's lying," I stammer. The force of her falsehood knocks me back on my heels. "Connor, please, not before the formal. I don't know what's happening, but we can fix it."

"See, that's the other thing Jenny told me." He whips around, pinning an icy stare on me. In the past two years as a couple, Connor's never once lost his temper on me, and my knees wobble at the switch in his temperament. "And you know, I think she's right. You care more about that formal than you do about our relationship, and I'm done with it all. It's like she said, you're not worth the hassle."

Connor's parting words are the final blow only Jenny knew they would be.

The one sentence that could unravel me and suffocate any fight I had left to save my relationship with Connor. My shoulders deflate as my feet remain glued to this one spot on the lawn. I don't pursue Connor anymore. Instead, I let him round the corner and disappear, out of sight.

If he sees the truth, why hold him captive?

Collapsing on a bench nearby, I huddle into myself and shiver against the frosty night air.

"There you are," a distressed voice sighs, catching its breath.

I pick my eyes up. An intense fire reignites in the pit of my stomach as Seth draws closer to the bench. "You." My anger flares with every step he makes toward me. "You did this."

"Excuse me?"

"Don't tell me you didn't come over as part of Jenny's plan."

"No, Madeline." Seth sticks his palms out toward me like he's trying to quell the rage, but I need to put it somewhere, and he's the perfect target. "I swear, I came to warn you. Something's off with Jenny."

"I don't care about Jenny, Seth!"

"Well, yes, you've made that clear, but I—"

"Why can't you leave me the fuck alone, huh?" I pick myself up from the bench and march toward him, stopping inches from his chest. "What the hell is it with you?"

"I don't know." He gives an agitated shake of his head before leveling a cutting glare in my direction. "I don't fucking know. You're like this goddamn infection poisoning my bloodstream." He lowers his voice until it becomes a rough whisper, sliding against my ears like warm sandpaper. My chest heaves against his, still so utterly frustrated that he ruined everything. For three years, I've worked tirelessly for this damn title, and Lumberjack Frasier is about to be the one to take me down.

"You terrorize every fucking part of me, Madeline Finch." He continues. "And trust me, if there were an antidote, I'd do whatever it takes to have it."

An infection.

A terror.

Not worth the hassle.

*Our little burden.*

That's what I am.

A burning sensation pricks my eyelids. In a blink, the wildwood of Seth's eyes quiets, shifting from agitation to a serene pasture, tender almost. "Maddie, no, please don't—*shit*." He brings his hand to my cheek, cradling it with his thumb, and wipes away a tear.

I lift my chin, a magnet drawing my lips ever closer to his.

"Go home, Seth," I whisper before I do something stupid. "You're not wanted here."

"Of course, I'm not. I'm not wanted anywhere," he mutters under his breath. He rubs the back of his neck, his green eyes still laser-focused on my face, before shaking his head and turning away. Pausing under the streetlight, he shoves his hands in his pocket and glances over his shoulder. "I'm sorry if I caused you any trouble tonight, Madeline. Believe me; it was unconsciously done."

For some inexplicable reason, my fingers yearn to reach for him, but I huddle back into myself and shed a few more tears.

*Ask him to stay.* It nettles my entire being, an itch I can't satisfy until I scratch it.

"Seth, wait."

Again, his trek forward halts.

I could ask him to stay.

I could apologize for letting my anger out on him instead of pointing the finger inward where it belongs.

I could be a better person.

"The um—the pictures."

His figure sags in the low light. "Already deleted. Don't worry."

"Oh. Okay. Thanks."

"Was that all?"

My teeth bare down on my bottom lip, biting back the invitation dancing on my tongue. "Yeah. That was all."

"Have a good night, Madeline," he says tenderly as if he's suddenly taken pity on me.

God, how pathetic must I look right now that *he's* pitying me?

"Night, Captain Pretentious," I say, trying to save face.

"Malibu Loki." He raises a peace sign in the air with his continued strides away.

My falsies grow heavy as I slink to the bench. With a pinch of my fingers, I rip them off and toss them in a nearby trash can before plopping back down on the slatted wood.

And then, wrapped under a blanket of twinkling stars, I let the tears run.

"Didn't know you could do that." A high-pitched voice slices through the bleakness. I jump, glancing around to find the figure to match the sound. The lady from the bookstore stands a few feet away, shuffling through the trash can like a feral raccoon.

"I didn't either," I mutter, not making eye contact with her. "What are you doing?"

"Trying to find your eyelashes," she says plainly as if picking through the trash for fake eyelashes is a totally sane thing. "Need them, I do."

"They sell falsies for like $5.99 at Ulta if you want a pack. I highly recommend getting them fresh."

"No, no, fresh won't do. I need the tears! A-ha!" she exclaims, raising two dead-caterpillar-looking lashes to the night sky in triumph. "Silly girl, do you know what I can do with these?"

"No offense, but I'm glad I don't."

With a click of her tongue, her eyes roam over me. "Oh yes, you have a big heart without all that frost, don't you? Put it in Jenny, of course, but she isn't handling it well. Too much for her. Her heart was smaller than yours, which surprised me too. But I can't just get rid of it. Oh, what a shame, though. You don't seem to have any love for yourself. Yes, that's where this all went wrong, isn't it, dear?"

I shift on the bench. People have reminded me my entire life how much of a burden I am. Why would I dare believe anything else without a title telling me differently? "There's not much to love."

"Oh, but there is—and you need to learn. No good to have a heart that big and have no room for yourself. Never mind, you'll learn tomorrow with your new story. Oh yes, a new start will do you well."

And with that, Ellie wanders away, leaving a crop dust of shimmers in her wake. Something cracks in my heart, like the last piece of ice is falling away. Another tear streams down my cheek. I wrap my arms around myself, guarding against the weird shifting winds. If only one of Jenny's bonkers theories could be right, just this once. Because a faerie writing me a new story sounds pretty damn glorious right now.

## CHAPTER FIVE
# The Princess Switch
### SETH

IT'S OFFICIAL. I shouldn't be allowed to socialize. Bad things happen when I try to people.

The person formerly known as Jenny Farrow draws a sip of her Peppermint Mocha latte through her nefarious smirk. The dim light of our go-to coffee shop on the edge of downtown shrouds her in an ominous shadow as she runs her fingers through the ends of her chestnut hair, curled and freed from the confines of her regular baseball cap.

Between her hairstyle and coffee order, our regular barista, Nancy, damn near had a heart attack.

In all our coffee adventures, Jenny's orders have remained the same. A large, hot black coffee. Because "why trouble people with extra work?"

I don't know if this change is a good thing. On the one hand, I'm proud of Jenny for ordering something she wanted. On the other, I'm worried that the order's a symptom of a more significant problem considering the shit she just pulled over Madeline and me.

"So, I think that all went pretty well, don't you?" she murmurs, inhaling the curls of steam wafting off the top of her mug. She brings her red-painted lips to the cup's brim for another sip, relishing her order.

And, if that question is a sign, she is also relishing the invitation she just received from Connor.

An invitation she orchestrated.

Yesterday, on my way home from Madeline's, I found out that Connor was never breaking up with her when his fist to my face and a brief conversation revealed the truth. Jenny made up some humorous lie about Madeline and me sneaking around and then backed it up with my shared location... at the exact time I was warning Madeline.

Catching Finch and me in our compromising situation was enough evidence to support Jenny's fabricated tale.

I shift on the bench, wanting to challenge Jenny's recent actions, but my head is too hazy with the whiplash of everyone's behaviors and my reaction to them.

I tried to comfort Madeline Finch last night.

What the hell was that?

The leather under my ass squeaks along with my nervous wiggle, making a terrible gas-passing sound, and I wait for Jenny's signature giggle and snort.

It doesn't come.

Fuck.

If she's not laughing at imitation fart sounds, she's truly gone to me.

Jenny flutters her mascara-covered lashes, peeking at me as if expecting a response to her statement. "Seth? Don't you think that went well?"

"I—" I stammer, the iridescent gloss over Jenny's eyelids further frying my circuits. I'm not against make-up or anything, but the symbolism behind Jenny wearing it now gnaws at me. It's the last sign I need to confirm that everything in my life has flipped on its head in the past five days.

Jenny's turning into Madeline, and with the way Madeline's softened, it feels like she's sucking her icy soul right out of her.

It makes little sense, but I swear they've been sliding into these new selves since that damn flicker of the lights in the toy store.

Or maybe even before when Jenny called Madeline by her given name and not her pet name, "Pookie," even though Madeline's tongue slipped and called her "Pixie" back.

I was expecting Jenny to cling to that moment forever. Instead, Madeline's now the enemy. Not that I mind. Jenny's always been too soft and needed better boundaries. But the way she's switched overnight from one extreme to the other? That's not okay. Evil never defeats evil. It just creates a bleak and hopeless situation for everyone.

"I don't appreciate being used as a pawn, Jenny," I say through gritted teeth. My fingers rake through the matted curls on top of my head, desperate for freedom from the beanie I always cover them with because I'd rather not bother with the routine my ex-girlfriend, Kennedy, had me maintain, but I'm not sure what to do with them otherwise.

Jenny dismisses my complaint with a shake of her head. "Oh, come on. You've hated Madeline more than me for years, and all we did was give her a taste of her own medicine."

"I still would've liked to have been consulted."

"I mean, you kind of were." She shrugs. "I didn't make you do anything. I just told you Connor was going to break up with her."

"Which was a lie." I pick up my glare, hoping my stony, grumpy façade will knock her out of whatever this is.

"Oops." She giggles with a smile. "Was it? I must have misunderstood him at the bookstore. Oh, I'm such a dumb bunny."

"I'm sure this was a misunderstanding, too. Huh?" I gesture to the swelling and bruising now shadowing my left eye.

"Oh no, Connor didn't appreciate finding you in Madeline's bedroom, so thank you for taking one for the team." She reaches out and pats my hand. A frosty bite pricks my skin on contact, and I recoil from her touch.

Where's the warmth that always radiates off every ounce of her?

"There's no team. This one is on you."

"I don't think so. If I remember correctly, you went to Madeline's house of your own free will, even though that's bizarre for someone to do when he hates the other person."

"I wanted to warn her." I fiddle with the knife from my place setting, rolling it between the pad of my thumb and my finger and focusing on the fluorescent light glinting off the cheap, soap-spotted metal. At least the half-hearted dishwashing at Slow Drip has the decency to remain the same.

"And why did you feel compelled to do that?" She cocks her head to the side.

"Because, for whatever reason, I couldn't stomach the thought of her getting hurt," I grumble.

"Hmm. I wonder if that has anything to do with the soulmate thing you laughed at me about."

"No fucking way." I shift again, sliding against the worn leather, Jenny's theory about soulmates and faeries stoking my dumpster fire of a rational mind.

There's no logical explanation for why I felt compelled to make sure Madeline didn't get hurt. Or how my heart shattered when I saw a tear roll down her cheek. It took every fiber of my being not to scoop her up and bring her back to her house, wrap her in a blanket, make her a hot beverage, and stay there until I knew she'd be okay again.

I dig the heel of my palms into my closed lids, regretting it when I press too hard on my bruise. God, I'm so fucked up that I can't even hate people correctly.

But magic, I guess—more than my social ineptitude would also explain why my best friend is possessed by the collective rabid spirit of every mean girl in a romantic comedy.

Whatever it is, the tornado of twirls and churns in my stomach tells me I shouldn't be here anymore, not when she's like this.

Vindictive, conniving, calculating her every social move—a Madeline clone.

"When you think about it, you're perfect for each other, her with her issues, and you with your tragic backstory. You're both so scared to let anyone in and hurt you."

With a glance up, the muscles between my brows bunch, puzzling out what Jenny means by any of that. "What issues?" I ask. "No, never mind. I don't want to know."

"You know what I'm referring to, anyway." She dismisses me with a wave of her hand and another delicate sip of her coffee.

I blink. Once. Twice. Maybe I can wake myself up from this nightmare. My jaw falls slack. Issues? Issues! That's what she's calling it?

Who is sitting in front of me, and where is my Jenny?

I lean over the table, seething with rage. "Are you fucking serious right now?"

Sophomore year, on my way out of class, I sensed something was wrong and wrapped my arms around Madeline before she cracked her head open on the sidewalk. I got her to the nurse's office, and they called Jenny, who was still her emergency contact person. After a week where I was "way too annoying," Jenny told me Madeline was okay and explained she had a disease called endometriosis that she didn't want anyone to know about.

I read a few journal articles I had access to on the disease because I'd never heard of it, and it's always good to be informed about the ways of the world.

It had nothing to do with my concern for Madeline Finch's well-being.

Absolutely not.

"Oh. I'm dead serious. Soon everyone else will know she's been hiding something from all the people she's supposed to love and trust, and our dear Madeline can see what it's like to have her friends leave her for a change."

"I can't talk to you when you're like this," I say in a huff, tugging my beanie back down over my head and exploding out of the booth.

"That's fine. Connor and I are meeting up soon, anyway." She hums, an evil grin peeking from behind her giant mug. "Yes, doing something for myself feels nice."

She doesn't mean just the coffee. "It's a slippery slope, Jenny," I mutter over my shoulder. "And when you get hit by karma or a truck, nobody will be there to pick you back up."

I slam my palms against the door's glass panes, rushing out into the mild Texas winter. The sun gleams down on me, and I roll my flannel sleeves to my forearms. It's too hot, and I'm too frustrated to suffer today. With a sigh, the swirled ink silhouette of me walking out onto a football field reveals itself on my lanky arms. Of course, I had to get a tattoo so complicated covering it is damn near impossible.

Ah, well. I bury that regret with many others, marching forward with one destination in mind.

The bookstore.

There isn't a problem in the world a good book can't help you ignore.

Do I have a TBR pile waiting in my dorm room large enough to fill an Olympic Swimming pool? Sure.

But part of buying a book and then reading it while your towering stack mocks you is that while you're reading, you worry about never catching up on your TBR instead of actual, real-life things. Like how your best friend's possessed.

It's better to worry about books than life.

Ten out of ten would recommend it.

I wouldn't have to worry if I were still a douche-canoe. But ah, well.

Things were so much simpler then. When all I had to do was play football and nothing else mattered. People were dying to be my friends. Kennedy was still in love with me, and I didn't know the cold reality of how much of my value lay in my ability to throw an egg-shaped leather ball.

My hand grips the cold brass knob of A New Chapter Bookstore, and I tug open the hard wooden door. A brief chill swirls around me, entering the store.

Hairs stand on the back of my neck. A shiver terrorizes my spine.

Shake it off.

There's probably a weird AC system here, judging by how old the place is.

My feet carry me on instinct to the New Releases Romance winter display. Without reading a single fucking blurb, I scoop up as many books as my arms can carry. If Jenny insists on this rabid personality, I will need something to support my impending reclusive lifestyle.

Romance books are always the answer.

A brown, tabby Bengal cuts across my path, and I wobble with my stash, barely making it to the counter before they avalanche out of my arms with a dramatic crash. I scan the store, searching for an employee, but I've yet to see one in the two times I've been here. Hopefully, the crash will draw someone's attention.

"Oh, he's here. Right on schedule!" A voice squawks from the back room. A woman with blonde hair piled high on her head blinks rapidly, entering behind the counter like she hasn't seen daylight in quite some time. Judging by the putrid scent emanating from her, she hasn't seen a soap bar, either. "Oh yes," she glances down at my pile of books. "You do like your romance novels. Don't you? I think that's your aura's doing—knows you were supposed to have this beautiful love story about healing, but Jack did you dirty, took that away from you."

My stomach twists itself into a knot. The word aura has been used far too much this week for my liking, but maybe even more concerning—how does this woman know about my affinity for romance novels?

I should leave and go to my usual bookstore. I don't know why I came here.

I just... did.

The lady makes a quick move in my introspection, lunging

towards my face with a pair of scissors, and I shut my eyes, ready to be massacred or something.

Her fingers tug on a strand of hair, pulling tight against my scalp. The snip of the scissor follows, and my alleged murder is over.

"What the—" My fingers tangle in my curls and find one significantly smaller than the rest.

"Hair makes the man." The Scissor Fiend exclaims.

Yeah, I should leave now. I step back on my heel. A careful, slow retreat shouldn't cause a ruckus.

"Oh yes, that's a good twist. I love it. He wants his old life back. We heard him say it, and he'd be such a good foil that way."

A floorboard creaks as I balance on my heel, frozen mid-step. I didn't say that out loud. Or remotely close to the store.

"I can read your thoughts, young man. I wrote them! Oh, yes, but that is the clever thing to do. Of course, this transformation will take some time, and sent her already we did. She'll get there first, but that's okay.

*Cut his hair,*
*Nice things to wear,*
*Heartbreak to heartbreaker,*
*Time again for Mr. Merrymaker.*
*Same people, different tale.*
*Time for you to tip the scale."*

The golden-haired lady chants in a haunting tone, sprinkling my curls around me on the ground.

I remain inert, unable to force movement to my leaden limbs.

Anxiety. It must be—a side effect of this bizarre interaction.

As an introvert, I never navigate social settings well. So when people deter from the usual "Hi, how are you? Crazy weather we're having today, huh?" small talk, I panic.

I need the formula.

And this—this isn't even an equation; this is a complete divergence from standard societal expectations.

You can't just cut somebody's hair and sprinkle it on the ground to verse! That's anarchy!

"Look," I squint, attempting to read the name tag obscured by the store clerk's salmon-colored cardigan. "Ellie, is it? Whatever is going on here—" I gesture to the hair seance thing around me. "I'm sure it's great, but I think I'm going to have to—"

A rumble through the dusty floorboards halts my exit speech. Books piled along the edge of various bookshelves rattle, falling to the floor in an organized, staccato rhythm. Ellie claps her hands, dancing to the beat.

"What the fuck?" I brace myself as the ground quake intensifies below me.

"Oh, you will be a prince among men once more, boy. Then you'll see to live without fear." She lifts her gaze with a cackle as a crack in the ground emerges and light blasts through, illuminating her in an eerie light.

"Oh. Before I forget! Can't see. Can't see! There are secrets down there!" She reaches into her pocket and grabs a fist full of something. She unfurls her fingers to reveal a mound of glitter.

"What are you—"

I can't finish my question before she blows on her hand, and gold dust clouds my vision. Twinkling silver and gold is the last thing I see before the ground drops out from underneath me, and I'm falling. I don't know whether it's falling to sleep or down a deep bottomless abyss. It feels strangely like both. Ellie shouting, "Don't fart in the hole. Faeries live down there," echoes with me in my lightless, slumbering void.

## CHAPTER SIX
# While You Were Sleeping
### MADDIE

THERE IS *a warm body pressed against my backside.*

I register the information as the heavy fog of slumber fades to dawning. My feet tangle in a flannel sheet, which I would say is unnecessary given the recent Texas climate, but there's a decided bite to the air in this room that suggests this cozy bedding is warranted.

It was a bit chilly last night. Maybe a cold front moved in while we—*I* was sleeping?

Right. The body.

It's probably not Connor's because he knows the rule about sleepovers and has never tried to break it.

I'm not a snuggler by nature, and I loathe sleeping in the same bed as someone else.

Morning breath.

Cold feet.

Frizzy hair.

Writhing in pain during a midnight flare.

Someone else seeing you at your most vulnerable?

Hard pass.

Calloused fingers graze my abdomen, and a radiant comfort

follows the soft caress. Then again, it could be Connor since his constant weightlifting has done a number on his hands.

Dammit. Re-establishing the "I don't snuggle" boundary will be difficult. He's always been too clingy for my taste, but ah, well. At least we made up, I guess.

Which... I don't remember.

Fresh pine swirls around me as the sheet of ice damming the memories in my mind cracks and floats away until a flood of memories rushes forward like white-capped rapids. But... they're wrong, somehow.

I rub my temple, hoping to clear my mind from its jumbled haze and tumultuous waves. Maybe if I open my eyes, clarity will find me.

Blinking, I squint against an ungodly light streaming through a pair of frosted windowpanes.

Okay, a cold front or not—that's impossible. It was seventy degrees yesterday afternoon.

*No. It was freezing like always in Balsam Hill.* A timid voice whispers in my brain.

*My* timid voice.

I thought I squashed that bit years ago.

Memories I swear are mine fade until they're nothing more than a faint whisper of a dream or a recollection of a movie I once watched. And a new set of memories, one that belongs to a more... sensitive... tender-hearted... wimpy... Maddie takes center stage.

Snowball fights with a bespectacled Connor.

Ice skating on a frozen cranberry bog in a Christmas tree farm.

A gazebo in the town square wrapped in Christmas lights and sparkling in the night sky.

A small college town with a quiet, rural, New England vibe to it.

Clutching a large hot chocolate while I navigate the icy

cobblestoned streets on campus and in town, banks of snow and icicles dripping from overhead awnings.

It feels like my life, but it's not. It can't be. I'm a Southern girl through and through, and I've never seen more than a dusting of snow, yet here I am, lying in bed with years and years of White Christmas memories screaming past my skull.

And *him*. The hand on my abdomen pulls me tighter against his warm chest.

A chest that doesn't belong to Connor.

Oh, no. It's a chest that belongs to someone far, far worse.

Seth I-was-pretentious-before-it-was-cool Aarons.

Terrified flutters bully the pit of my stomach at the contact.

*Oh yes, a new start will do you well.* Ellie's parting words voice-over the holiday-worthy montage playing in my mind. Between the host of fresh memories and my presence in the bed of the last man on Earth I'd be caught dead with, I don't have it in me to be skeptical anymore.

Either A. Jenny was right, and faeries are real.

And very vindictive, considering my current situation.

Or B. I did a massive amount of drugs last night.

I'm not sure which reality I'd prefer.

Faeries, maybe?

It would be one hell of a trip otherwise.

Whatever the explanation, I should leave this room. Fast.

With all the stealth and grace I can muster and a bit of lady-like grunting, I roll toward the edge of the bed. Almost. There.

Seth's arm tightens, and with a little squeal, all the space I procured disappears, and I'm pressed against his warm chest again.

"Stay," he murmurs into my hair.

My limbs relax with the command, compelled to comply.

But my brain remains Team-Get-The-Fuck-Out.

For whatever reason, Seth is a craving my body is desperate to indulge in, and well, I like my dignity, thanks.

"I need to study for a final." I inch my way toward the edge of the bed again, freeing myself from his arm. "Go back to sleep."

"I'll help you study after breakfast."

"Liar," I say. If my memory serves me right, and let's be honest, I'm not keen on trusting it; every time this man has claimed to "help" me study, I've ended up on my back, begging for him. It was enough of a blow to my ego to wake up here. I don't need to live out one of our disgustingly common, high-strung sexcapades.

My toes press against the hardwood floor, and I wince at the freezing sensation that terrorizes the soles of my feet.

Crawling back into the warm comfort of that bed grows more alluring with every tortured step.

What kind of psychopath lives in a place where the floor hurts your feet?

I grab my t-shirt thrown across the workout bench with a groan, retro band t-shirts are so not my vibe, but I know instinctively that this is mine, and since I, unfortunately, slept without clothes last night, I'll have to accept it. I toss it over my head. The quicker I am dressed, the quicker I can get answers.

A new start sounded great in my desperation, but all of this? With him? Wearing... vintage band t-shirts and... flannel? I won't ever be *this* desperate.

My pants and socks are thrown near a desk that has seen a lot of extra-curricular activity this semester. A shiver terrorizes my spine, whether, at the vivid recollections of what's been done to me on that wooden slab, or the freezing temperatures of this room, I don't know.

I could sneak back into bed.

Wait, what? No.

Get the hell out of this room.

Slinging my pants over my shoulder for dressing on the go, I tiptoe towards the door.

It'll be safer to put them on in the hallway, away from him.

"Maddie?" a groggy voice mumbles.

My hand remains extended towards the knob, eager to vacate this room. "Yes, Seth?" I sigh.

"Why the hell are you leaving my room without pants on?"

"I didn't want to wake you," I say, nervous energy spiraling inside.

*Because I want to pounce on you and then spend the day curled up against your side, and I have this suspicious feeling that if I glimpse at you, I won't have the willpower to save myself.*

"It's a little late for that."

"Oh, well—" I shrug, out of excuses, but still desperate to vacate the premises. The intoxicating scent of pine and cedar swirls a hand around me. Something begs me to curl back into bed with Seth. Like there's an unrelenting tug between us that I can't quite explain.

I reach again for the knob. There's no way I'm dealing with these sensations, and there isn't a moment to spare regarding Operation Get-Ellie-To-Undo-This and Operation-Learn-How-to-Murder-aeries.

Hopefully, it's something as easy as killing vampires with garlic, but even if it's a tad trickier, I'll devote my entire life to the mission.

Because me? Enamored with Lumberjack Frasier? Really?

And the fantasies I've had of him, too.

This Maddie is pathetic.

"Buttercup, please don't go out there like that," Seth groans. "I don't want to fight all the guys this early."

With a heavy sigh, I relent. My fresh memories of this timeline tell me that Seth is the star quarterback of some D1 college in New Hampshire—Fezziwig University. And he lives with a bunch of his teammates in an old, drafty colonial house on campus.

So exiting this room without pants isn't a great idea either.

But I'm a mature young lady with plenty of grace and self-control. I can put my pants on here without jumping Seth Aarons's bones.

I am calm, cool, and unaffected by the man lying in bed.

Gathering the rough denim, I slip my leg in. Seth shifts in bed. My eyes draw to him with the feedback from the sliding friction. The top sheet falls just enough to catch a peek at the broad, toned chest that singed my shoulder blades minutes earlier. Ink swirls around a chiseled pectoral and down a muscular, veined arm, and that's all it takes to annihilate my will to leave. Every inch of me wants to laugh. Captain Pretentious would never mar his body like that.

And he'd hate that Ellie's made him a one-dimensional jock, who fucks and plays football phenomenally, but needs a tutor.

Needs *me*.

In my shameful ogling, I miss my second pant leg and tumble to the floor with a yelp.

"Jesus, you okay?" He bolts upright in bed, and the sheet drops to his lap.

Oh hell. My goal to get dressed without jumping Seth Aarons suffers damaging blows with his exposed chest. Light streams in from the window, falling on his soft, pillow lips twisted into a worried frown and highlighting his dimpled chin. Auburn tendrils wink in the morning light, buried in his chestnut curls tousled to perfection on top of his head and shaved short on the side.

He lazily runs his fingers through them—his biceps flex. The skin over the ridges and valleys of his abdomen pulls taut.

It's doubtful he knows how sinfully sexy he is right now.

But I sure the hell am.

A corner of his mouth tugs up ever-so-slightly, and his verdant gaze twinkles with mischief.

Never mind, he's fully aware, too.

Maybe shamelessly staring at him from the floor without a modicum of pride or chill tipped him off.

This is retribution for every past evil deed I've ever committed. It must be.

There's no other way to explain the fluttering, sputtering

insides yelling that I'm the property of Seth Aarons or the crystal-clear revelation that ownership doesn't run both ways.

I'm Seth Aarons's fuck buddy, and we both know it.

"Can you just come back into bed, Buttercup?" he asks, his voice still thick with sleep. "Or I can throw you over my shoulder and put you back here; however you want to play it?" He flashes a devilish grin, and any self-control I possess evaporates in the blaze hung in his cheeky gaze.

"Fine, you win," I huff, extricating my leg from my pants and crawling back into bed like the pitiful, spineless worm I am.

"I knew I would," he says, smug and satisfied. His hand ventures under the soft cotton of my shirt and rests flat on my abdomen—curls of excitement spiral from my head to my toes with the brief contact. On instinct, I wrap my feet around his. "That's a good girl," he murmurs into my hair.

Slowly, Seth lifts his hand, trailing a finger up my sternum, and cups one of my breasts, running the pad of his thumb across my nipple.

*Oh.*

Warmth pools in between my thighs, and I steady my breaths, eager not to turn around and show how much a simple graze of his thumb is affecting me.

A tiny, imperceptible whimper escapes my lips, and my feet move up and down his calf.

I'm not proud, but I also don't have control of whatever feelings his touch is eliciting. I need more.

"Just let me sleep a little longer, and I'll take care of you. I'm sorry, I'm still on West Coast time after that game," he trails off. His chest rises and falls with the heavy cadence of slumber, and I cling to the rhythm of his breaths to literally calm my tits.

In his dormant state, I take stock of every sensation—magnified in a way I never experienced with Connor. Pine swirls around me, calling to me like it's claimed me. Embers spark along my skin at every point of contact. For the first time, my body relaxes into someone else's embrace. It feels like coming home with a surrendering sigh after a long day away or the feel of a hot cup of tea on a rainy day.

A quiet, glorious comfort.

It should terrify me. And oh, it does. My brain is that dog GIF with the surrounding fire drinking coffee and going, "this is fine." But my body is charged with some euphoric, divine, incandescent feeling. Like I swallowed the moon, and now moonbeams are going to shoot out of my fingers and toes.

Shit. I've heard about this feeling. This Maddie is in love.

# CHAPTER SEVEN
# Trading Places
### SETH

**THERE IS A PEBBLED** *nipple under the pad of my thumb.*

I don't know who it belongs to, how I came to share a bed with them, or even when this happened. But I know without a doubt that my hand is now cupping the world's most perfect breast. *How did Adam Carlsen get his mouth around one of these?* Never mind that, right now. My thumb draws circles around the sensitive peak, and the tiny whimper accompanying each swirl is the sweetest fucking music to my ears.

Even if I can't remember who it is.

What *do* I remember about last night?

Drinking?

I got coffee with Jenny at the diner.

Is this Jenny?

My gut's telling me no, whatever she was morphing into wouldn't lower herself to plain old boring Seth Aarons.

After the diner, I went to the bookstore.

And some old lady blew powder into my face.

Did she drug me?

Reluctantly, I lift my fingers from the gorgeous breast and roll to the side of the bed to sit up. A frigid floor freezes the soles of my feet when I press them to the ground. This isn't my dorm room since that floor's carpeted. I grind the heels of my palms into my eyelids to clear the haze of sleep and wince, waiting for the pain that rubbing my black eye should elicit, but it never comes.

"What the fuck?" I whisper, blinking my eyes open and squinting through a blinding light. The room I'm in, with its white walls and old, hardwood floors, doesn't match the Ephron University 1990s vibes for off-campus housing or anything else around this area, but it's still familiar, just not in any logical sense. With the weight bench in the corner, and the athletic shorts flung everywhere, there's a nostalgic feel of my former life hanging heavy in the chilly air.

What the hell is this? My brain and processing system remain murky, held hostage by a thick sludge.

"Hey, you okay?" A soft voice wraps me in a velvety cocoon, drawing small circles on my back, and I tense at the surprise contact.

There's a lilt that I recognize, but it can't be because that voice has never been soft—and why would she be in my bed, anyway?

With a slow turn, I meet a pair of cerulean eyes, sparkling and comforting, like the warm sun hanging in the afternoon sky. No frost. No chill. All pleasantness.

I rub my temple with my forefinger, trying to eradicate the haze that doesn't want to clear. "Maddie?" I croak.

"I'm here," she whispers with an unfamiliar gentleness. Yeah, I'm definitely dreaming. "Let's get you laying back down. You look like you've seen a ghost or something."

"Yeah, or something." I scrub my hands down my face. *Wake up. Wake up.*

Over the years, I've never been able to handle any form of interaction with Madeline Finch after these far-too-frequent nightmares.

She always dominates me in them.

Always has me on my knees, desperate for her. Like every ounce of me belongs to her.

And if Madeline Finch ever caught a whiff of my subconscious... that there's a part of me that would follow her along like an obedient, love-stricken puppy if she ever turned her attention to me affectionately... I'd be screwed.

She'd do it to mess with and shatter me without question.

With a delicate pull on my shoulder, she lowers me back down to my pillow, my back sighing with relief as it meets the mattress.

"There? Is that better?" she asks, wiping beads of sweat that have collected over my furrowed brow.

"Uh, yeah. Thanks." I clear my throat, bringing my gaze to hers. In an instant, I am sucker-punched by everything I loved the first few times I saw Maddie. Her hair, its natural color, a golden halo around her pale, freckled face. The pink pouty lips I've thought about kissing and leaving red and puffy more times than I care to admit. Her button nose.

When I saw her like this, I knew that she, more than anyone I've ever met, had the power to obliterate me.

I thought about approaching and introducing myself to her, doubtful she even knew I existed.

But then, she beat me to it, introducing herself at a party, dressed in an outfit ingrained in my memories because Kennedy had me take a good forty photos of her in it for her Instagram. Everything screamed inside as she extended her hand, and mine shook, frozen in fear by my side. I'd suffered enough destruction and barely made it out alive. Madeline Finch was not a chance I was willing to take.

So I told myself, "No." We weren't doing this. (In my stupor, I may have said that word out loud, but I doubt she heard me.) And then downed a glass of punch I saw someone spike with a heavy hand a few moments earlier.

It's a decision I never regretted after witnessing how cruel Madeline was, dropping Jenny without so much as saying a word to her.

But here, this is the Maddie I saw the first few times—occasions where I didn't work up the courage to make my presence known.

The first time she was broken, crying in the kitchen, making herself a cup of tea while I was over at Jenny's for a study session. My eyes danced over her, and my body hummed like it was sparking alive after years of living in anticipation. Jenny's never let me forget it because I sat, transfixed, mouth agape, and the words "holy shirtballs, that is the most beautiful woman I have ever seen" escaped past my lips.

And the second, a week later, Jenny invited me to meet them both at a diner for milkshakes. I froze in the doorframe. My heart sputtered, and I chickened out. Being in her orbit was too risky, so I never joined them, choosing to protect my heart instead.

My hand reaches toward her, tracing the curve of her jaw. "God, you're beautiful." The words leave my mouth low and hushed. But what does it matter? This isn't real, anyway. Nothing I say can be held against me in Dreamland.

Pink gathers on Maddie's cheeks, and I grin. Her blush may be one of my favorite things. Even when we're fighting, it's my constant companion after all these years — the acknowledgment that no matter how cool she's playing it on the outside, I still get to her too.

"Especially when you blush for me," I growl, rolling her on her back as a strange sensation—or knowledge that between these sheets, Madeline Finch is mine—emboldens me. Maybe this dream will be different.

"You promised you'd take care of me when you woke up, not hover and torture me." She squirms, reaching for me.

"They aren't the same thing?" I ask with a smirk.

Maddie's brow dips into the scowl I've grown accustomed to, and I press a kiss on the tensed muscle on her forehead. As if my lips were the key, it relaxes in an instant with an accompanied, glorious sigh.

Yeah, this dream is definitely different. Thank you, unconscious Seth, for doing something for yourself for a change, buddy.

"There's a good girl. I'm sorry I kept you waiting for so long. Thank you for being so patient."

*She has a praise kink.* Again, it's drilled into me like these are things I know from experience. She has a few other kinks, too—places to touch her that drive her crazy, but there's something that I know about this Maddie that, if I were still on the fence, would solidify my dream theory.

Because the real Madeline Finch would never tolerate it.

My lips hover near her other cheek, my breath tickling against her skin. I trace her jaw with my nose before rising to her earlobe and dragging my teeth down the lower portion of it. "Beg for me, Maddie," I whisper harshly.

The surprise catch in her throat almost destroys me right there. I want to shout—*I'll do anything you fucking want to make that sound again.* But that won't get Dream Maddie off.

Instead, I tug on the collar of her shirt, exposing her collarbone. My finger traces along the ridge, and I blow hot air everywhere my finger travels.

She shivers underneath me. "Seth," she says with a dramatic exhale.

I groan, struggling to contain myself. "My name sounds so much sweeter coming off your lips when you're like this." With a soft graze of my fingers, I follow the hem of her underwear, relishing the delicious friction between my rough callouses and her smooth skin.

Maddie whimpers underneath me.

"Beg for me, Maddie, and I'll do whatever the hell you want."

"P-please." She closes her eyes, burying her lower lip behind the whites of her teeth.

"Please, what?" I drag my finger back up over her sternum, tracing the rosy peaks of her breast.

"Touch me." The request comes out as nothing more than a strained whisper.

"I'm not already doing that?" I reach a hand down to the inside of her knee, traveling toward her thigh, driven with a desire to watch this glacial woman melt under my touch. To make her just as much a breathless, heart-hammering, whimpering mess as I was when I first saw her.

Maddie's breathing slows as I draw ever closer to where she wants to be touched, and I halt in the crook of her thigh, her skin scorching my fingertips with every small circle I trace there.

"Seth, I need you. Please."

"Please, what, Maddie? What do you want me to do?"

"Okay, seriously?" That glorious whimper hits my ears again, and I'm a fucking goner. As cool as I know I have to play this for her; seeing her like this, undone in my bed, it's fucking dangerous. No way in hell I can face the real Madeline after this. "Fuck me with your fingers. I'm begging you."

A low, satisfied chuckle rumbles in my chest. "I guess if you're so desperate, I could put you out of your misery." I tease. Reaching my nightstand, I grab a bottle of oil I keep there just for her.

It's a CBD oil designed for people with pelvic pain to help their muscles relax during intimacy and a targeted ad that frequently appears on my browsers. I swear, you google one or five things about endometriosis and read romance novel blogs, and your targeted ads go from protein drinks to CBD arousal oil.

Opening the bottle, I drop some onto my fingers. "Slide your underwear down for me and show me where you want to be touched."

Warmth coils deep in my belly as Maddie listens, hooking her fingers in her waistband and pulling her underwear down. She circles her clit, her back arching at the light contact. "Shit," she hisses.

"There you go, good girl," I murmur. "Do you feel how ready you are for me?"

"Mhm." She buries her lips again behind the whites of her teeth, and I'm tempted to dip down and suck her bottom lip back out, coaxing her to let go of any modicum of restraint she's still pretending to have.

Instead, I dip my head to her breasts, and my tongue lashes against her stiff, sensitive peaks. "My turn to feel," I say, blowing hot air down her sternum. Maddie moves her hand, and I sink a finger with the oil into her entrance, gently swirling and then dragging the wetness and the oil up to her clit, reveling in the heat surrounding me and the tiny sigh of relief that passes over her lips.

Her breathing turns heavy as I circle the edge of her bundle of nerves, giving the oil time to soak in.

"Okay, seriously?" Her arms extend toward me in a desperate grab to pull me against her. "We get it. I'm desperate for you. Congratulations. Come here so I can kiss you while you fuck me."

With a disapproving click of my tongue, I wrap a firm hand around her delicate wrists and pin them over her head. "Patience, Buttercup."

I zero my focus in on the rhythm of her reaction to my finger inside of her, swirling it on her center until she bucks against it, bringing her close to the edge but never over it.

"I—Seth—shit." She tilts her head, trying to capture my lips as I bury them into the side of her neck, relishing the intoxicating rosewater scent and her hammering pulse.

Something warm and devious sparks in my chest at her neediness. "Do you know how long I've wanted you wrapped around my finger like this, Maddie? Begging for a kiss from me." With a brush of my nose, I trace her jaw, coming close to her lips but never touching them.

She shivers when I press a kiss on the inside of her collarbone.

Continuing my exploration of her body, I take her pebbled nipple into my mouth. Her back arches as she cries out a simple "fuck."

"Seth, pressure. Please."

It's not time to give in. If I drive her further, it'll be worth it for both of us.

"Say you're mine, Maddie, and I'll do whatever you want to release you."

Super douchey. But it's what she needs to get there.

The beautiful whimper hits my ears again. Her teeth rake across her lower lip like she's almost weighing her options.

"Imyours"

It's a soft, incoherent grumble.

"I'm sorry, I don't think I quite got that," I say with a shake of my head. I move over to the other breast, resting neglected for far too long.

"Please."

"Say the words coherently. That's all you have to do." My tongue flicks against her swollen, sensitive pink peak.

"Shit." She writhes under me as I move to a pulsating rhythm against her bud. Her fingers clutch into my hair, and I feel the last bit of her reserved demeanor fall away from her. "I'm yours, Seth, okay?"

"Fucking right you are," I growl, gently removing my finger from her and wiping it on my lips. "Do you want to taste how mine you are, Maddie?"

She nods, eyes narrowed on my lips with unrestrained, heated intensity. Feral. That's what the Ice Queen's melted away to.

I lean in and let my lips brush hers, savoring how she parts them the moment mine capture hers.

But Maddie isn't in the mood for savoring anything, and soon she's devouring my mouth as if she's a woman who's been starved for years for a kiss rather than the few minutes of extended torture she's endured. A beat of surprise at the hunger of her embrace shifts the tables. No longer in control, I'm held captive by the sweet feel of her lips against mine and the curl of heat that wraps around my body pressed close to her.

Nothing has ever been more intoxicating than holding Madeline Finch on the edge. Watching her unravel because of my touch, it's a power I didn't know I craved, but hell, I'll crave it forever now, even if this is a dream.

With full addiction imminent, I pull away from her lips, careful not to betray who's running the show here.

Even like this, she's dominating me. I'm possessed with the

need to see her come undone underneath me. Driven with that desire—I'll go mad if she doesn't let me, I know it.

I narrow my eyes on hers, and with a slow drag of my fingers, I wet two of them in my mouth. Her breath hitches. Pupils dilate. And I'm hooked.

"You want these?" I ask.

"Please," she gasps.

"So polite for me." I grin, circling her entrance before dragging them in and out. She bucks against my fingers with a surrendering moan, and I watch transfixed as her breath grows faster and more erratic. She loses herself to sporadic cursing and back arching. Her eyes are wild and unguarded, like a vast ocean threatening to capsize a ship with its violent waves. A warm form of possession takes over me as she lies beneath me. God, she's beautiful like this.

A long, climactic cry pulls me out of my haze of admiration. Maddie arches her back one final time, falling against the mattress in quiet resignation. "Fuck, I'm yours," she says, wiping her sweat-slicked hair out of her face and not meeting my eyes. Like it's a regretful part of her reality.

"There are worse things you could be," I whisper, gently capturing her lips, desperate to reassure her. *We're playing, darling. You're safe with me.* I want to say.

But this is a dream, so what use are those words?

"Doubtful," she says against my lips. "But it's okay. Everything will be back to normal soon."

Sub-conscience translation: Seth, get your act together because you're going to wake up soon, and the real Maddie is nothing like this, and if you're not careful, she still has the power to destroy you.

"But Seth?" Maddie whispers.

"Yes, love?"

"You think you could—would you mind...." She bites her lip, at war with herself over her request.

"Whatever it is, Maddie, I'll do it. Just ask."

"Could you snuggle me?" It's a low, embarrassed murmur, but that request has the power to smash my heart wide open.

"Of course, Buttercup." I press my lips against her forehead, rewarded with eyelids that flutter closed and a soft smile on contact. Fuck. I could kiss this woman's forehead forever. Slowly, I turn her on her side, wrapping my arms around her.

Her feet meet my calf with a satisfied hum. "I didn't know it could feel like this."

"What?"

"Snuggling. I—it feels different when it's with you, that's all."

The warm flutters in the lower portion of my stomach, which have always turned into screaming aches whenever Madeline Finch is around, would agree with that assessment. Touching her is unlike anything I've ever experienced. It's like a warm fire crackling in the hearth, this comfort of home when it's contained, but there's always the threat that if I let it grow, it could consume and burn me alive. It's spellbinding, and for the first time, it doesn't feel like a curse.

I lay my palm flat on her taut stomach, savoring our tangled heat. "I get that," I say against her hair. Rosewater locks lull me into a false sense of safety.

But I'll enjoy it since dreams like these don't last forever.

## CHAPTER EIGHT
# Let it Snow
### MADDIE

THE BELL PERCHED over A New Chapter's entrance rings with urgency as I slam open the door and stomp over the bookstore's dusty threshold with one goal: get Ellie to undo everything. "You made me Seth Aarons's booty call?" My voice thunders over the persistent chime.

Present life a mess or not, there's no way I'm letting three years of hair appointments, curating the perfect wardrobe, cuticle care, and social climbing go to waste.

I'd much prefer to remain "Satanic Barbie" in a dire situation than be "Tutor Girl" because, oh, yeah, that's my nickname here.

*Pathetic.*

My converse thud with every heavy, angry footstep toward the weathered counter. For all the differences around me, all the brick colonial buildings and snow-covered chimneys, this place remained the same.

The winter display winks, laughing at me, and I peer at a new title I missed on my last visit, a picture of a man in a grey beanie and a flannel gazing down at a blonde-haired woman in a pink peacoat with an uncanny resemblance to myself on the cover.

No. It can't be—

I reach towards it.

"Spoilers. Maddie. Spoilers are no good." A voice tsks behind me, and I jump, retracting my hand.

Ellie stands, unblinking, behind the counter.

"*Love at Frost Sight*? You couldn't think of anything better?"

"I don't name them." She shrugs. "I write the stories. Different faerie binds them and makes the story permanent."

"It's a lot skinnier than the other ones." I grab the book, studying it from multiple angles. An already published story may impede my Have-Ellie-Undo-This strategy, but maybe where it's skinnier, she won't mind.

I'm saying there's a chance, anyway.

"It's a novella. Holiday ones are all the rage now, you know, but... you both don't need much to get to where you were supposed to be, just a push and a fresh start where you don't have all that compounding anxiety on your shoulders."

"Yeah, so about this fresh start," I say nervously. The matte cover of the book sparks like hot coals against my fingers, and I cram it back on the display rack.

"Yes, you're welcome for that. Don't you feel much better, girl?"

"No. I feel the exact opposite of better. I think you may have confused helping me with torturing me, so if you wouldn't mind, please undo... all of this." I gesture at myself. "Now." I cross my arms, hoping I can still muster a cutting glare, but I fear my stare's about as sharp as a butter knife. Darn.

She licks the tip of her pencil and jots down a note, hand flying in a possessed writing frenzy. "Won't do. Helping or torturing, whatever you want to call it, the story's finished, so there's no use trying to wiggle your way out of it now. Once I start a story, I need to see it through, or the noggin gets too full of voices." She taps her pencil with her head. "It won't do to have a lot going up here."

"That's not happening already?" I snort.

The pencil falls out of Ellie's grasp with a decided sigh. She raises her feline eyes, meeting mine. "Even without the frost, you've always been a stubborn one. Wanting to do whatever you want, never following the outline I curated for your life. That's why Jack could manipulate the storyline because I couldn't get a good grip on you two. But I figured it out, and it's a different feel for a story than I normally do, so I'm determined to see it through. Deal with it."

"What if I refuse to comply?" I'm not sure I have free will or if the story is truly permanent, but Ellie's agitated stare at this question suggests that maybe faeries have a different definition of the word permanent, and I have some say. "I still have some free will, don't I? I'm not just a character device."

"Yes," she sighs. "There's still room to mess up your beautiful story, which I don't recommend. So, tell you what, girl. I'll make a deal with you." Her lips tip into a crooked grin. The hairs stand on edge on the nape of my neck. My gut screams that I shouldn't make deals with a faerie, but right now, I have little actual power, so I might as well listen to her.

"I'm listening." I pick at an imaginary piece of lint and pluck it off my shirt to Ellie's condescending snort. "What?"

"Nothing. You reminded me of another pain in my ass who bumbled around his soulmate, too. But never mind, here's the deal. Get that boy Seth to fall in love with you again before you return to your world on Christmas Day, and I'll give you ten minutes of your actual life to redo." She reaches for something behind the counter, placing an hourglass on the wooden slab. A miniature house and a frosted fir tree sit inside on a mountain of white glitter.

"*A blizzard will start when you win back his heart.*
*The past, it will take you for one ten-minute redo.*"

"You will fart when you eat a gluten-filled tart." I mimic the enchanting lilt of Ellie's voice and fidget at the ridiculous nature of all of this.

"What?" Ellie snaps her head up as her hand circles the top of the hourglass.

"Uh, nothing. I'm just considering your deal."

"And you make jokes when you're uncomfortable instead of biting people's heads off now. That's right. Forgive me, I forgot."

"That's fine... I guess..." I pull at my fingertips. Could I even do anything within ten minutes? It's not like that's a tremendous amount of time. But maybe it's enough to stop Seth from entering my room. Without him there, Connor wouldn't have broken up with me, and then we'd still be together for the formal.

And I wouldn't lose everything I've worked so hard for.

Honestly, what do I have to lose except some alternate reality dignity? It's not like anyone else here is even aware that there's a world with another Maddie who would be mortified to see and do any of this.

"Ellie, you have a deal," I say, extending my hand for a shake. Oh, on second thought, I retract my offer. "I have one condition, though."

"Always the pain in my ass. What is it, child?"

"I need you to take it easy on these feelings. I can't seduce Seth if I'm a nervous wreck whenever he's around."

The bells on Ellie's festive sweater jingle with a decided shake of her head. "I can't control the intensity of your feelings, dear. Every soulmate bond is different, but you two have a special one. You've just never felt it without that frost in your heart. That's why you're having such a hard time."

"Then why isn't this Seth falling at my feet, too? Shouldn't it go both ways?"

"Had Jack put some frost in him. Just enough to teach you a lesson. You can't have everything easy here. You were a piece, you know. But don't worry. Get it to melt, and he'll be a goner like you."

Captain Pretentious, with tattoos and a six-pack falling at my feet? Really fucking tempting.

A sharp pain twinges on my left side, it's been stabbing me since Seth and I were intimate yesterday, which isn't a complete surprise. I always flared after Connor and I did that sort of thing, but where it didn't hurt too much while Seth and I were intimate, I was hoping maybe I'd be okay after as well.

Apparently, I'm not. And the pain is getting to where I can't ignore it.

"Okay, but did you have to give this to me in this life, too?" I ask with a crunch.

"Yes, unfortunately." Ellie frowns, peering at me without any judgment or malice. "Human bodies are different. I can't manipulate them as easily as the soul. That is a part of you in every reality. All I could do was encourage this Maddie to stay up on her pelvic exercises and write Seth so he knows how to be intimate with someone with your disease. You're welcome for that." She peeks up, a dance sparkling in her eye, and—lord, this is uncomfortable.

"Yup. That's my cue to get the hell out of here! Thanks for making this awkward as always!" I grab the magical hourglass thingy and step back on my heel, heading toward the front door.

"Yes, I've stalled you long enough. Now is the perfect time to leave." She claps her hands to my worrying frown, and I bust out the door to the frigid New England air.

**THE LOCAL COFFEE SHOP,** Cup of Cheer, has the world's best salted caramel hot chocolate. That's what the sign on the window boasts, anyway. And I'm desperate to try the beverage of choice I consume in an alarming volume in this reality.

Boughs of pine hang along the black iron rafters, sheltering a wooden ceiling. Edison lights dangle at various heights, shining bright against an otherwise dark brick wall.

"Here you go, Maddie." A college student smiles behind the counter, a dimple winking on his cheek. Zach. His name is Zach.

Old wooden floors groan under my steps as I walk to the

counter and accept the disposable mug with a Christmas sweater print resting in his hands.

"Thanks!" I squeak, shifting on my heels. Wrapping my hands around the cup, I take a moment and relish the warmth that embraces them in return. Everything from this welcome heat and Zach's greeting is the best kind of Chicken Soup for the Soul-cozy, and I relax into the sensations rather than stand on guard in my usual attack mode.

"How's studying for your finals going?" I ask, inhaling the curls of steam wafting off the top. I don't know if I've ever been more content.

Which is alarming because, with my appearance, I haven't been this vulnerable in public in years.

I'm wearing the same band shirt from yesterday. My hair is a frizzy-I-had-sex mess, and nothing is hiding the finals-week bags under my eyes. And yet, Zach seems happy to converse with me, like none of those things matter.

"Finals are going pretty well. Someone made me this killer study guide, and it's been wicked helpful," he says, wiping down a spot on the counter with a white dish towel.

I almost snort at the New England colloquialism slipped in but catch myself. It's supposed to be normal for me.

"Whoever did that sounds amazing!"

"I think so." He flashes a cheeky grin, resting his forearms on the counter and peering at me. "You working at the tree farm today?"

"Oh, um." I search my memories. Images emerge of me working at a frozen cranberry bog-turned-skating rink in a Christmas tree farm called "Pining All the Way." A shiver works down my spine. So that explains my terrible hot chocolate addiction, then. "Yeah, I have one of my Humanities classes with Professor Calvin in a bit, and then I'll be over to start my shift."

"Great, I'll see you over there." Zach flips his towel over his shoulder. "Threw a few extra marshmallows and whipped cream in there if you want to return the favor later." He winks.

I pause. Am I—with Zach, too?

Recalling our former interactions, they're of him working on his slapshot on the bog while I close for the day.

Oh. So that's what he means. Skating. The favor is extra skating time. Fair trade for marshmallows and whipped cream.

"Sure, I'll see you there." I awkwardly tip my cup at him before turning around with a grimace to leave the shop. I need to learn how to socialize again because dorky isn't a good look.

Outside, I breathe in the frigid air, wincing as it clutches my lungs in its firm grip.

In my justifiable rage marching over to the bookstore an hour ago, I didn't take stock of everything going on in the center of town. But now, all I have is time before class and work. Since I've never seen snow or a town that—if the founding date of 1638 on the "Welcome to Balsam Hill" sign is accurate—is older than the actual country, I should take a second and appreciate whatever I can.

Fleecy snowflakes drift overhead. I tilt my head up, admiring the snow globe-frosted sky. A few flakes catch my eyelashes, and others dust my peacoat with icy crystals, sparkling in the light of a nearby cast-iron, Victorian streetlamp graced with a giant wreath of balsam fir.

I head toward my apartment, which sits over the local college bar, The Brazen Blitzen. Connor's my roommate and my best friend in this world.

My converse thud against the cobblestoned streets, narrowed by banks of shoveled snow. A subtle breeze wraps its freezing hand around my cheeks. With another wintery gust, something creaks. It's a sign hanging out in front of Hermey's Dentistry, now swaying, its hinges whining with the back-and-forth movement. I pause, reading the sign, and let another sip of hot chocolate warm my throat.

*Why did the cookie come to the dentist? Because he had gingervitis.*

With a laugh, I choke on my sip. *Ellie, you have too much time to think.*

Pinecones, branches, and holly berries burst out of birch logs and various mason jars adorning a display window of the florist shop sitting next to Hermey's—Zuzu's Petals. Yellow lights twinkle along the edge of the store, with boughs of garland and a wreath decking the brick facade and several other buildings along the street. Twinkling icicle lights zigzag overhead across Main Street. Memories of staring up at them as I am now and wishing upon the winking stars warm my insides in a way my hot chocolate could never manage.

My eyes stay glued skyward while I stride forward.

*Make Seth fall in love with you again.*

*Again.*

*Win back his heart.*

What the hell did Ellie mean when she said those words? Did she misspeak? I mean, she had to, right?

Because all Seth Aarons has ever done is hate me in my world, and he doesn't seem too interested in any emotional attachments in this one, either.

*Oof.*

My body meets a hard wall of muscle, and my lid flies off. Hot chocolate sloshes out of my cup with the sudden braking.

"Fuck. That's hot." A voice hisses, sucking in a large gulp of air through their teeth.

"I'm so sorry. I wasn't—" Common sentence structure eludes me when I meet a familiar pair of green eyes. A pair that twinkled with power yesterday, watching me unravel underneath him. I snuck out this morning, hoping never to see him again, but now that I have to make him fall in love with me, that plan is as out the window as I was at seven a.m. "I wasn't watching where I'm going."

"Neither was I." He shakes his head. His lips curl into the hint of a smile. "A lot to look at today, huh?"

Which, I'll admit, is a weird thing to say when, as far as I can tell, this town has looked like this at Christmas for the entire four years we've been at this school.

"Um, yeah." I dab at the stain with a spare napkin I used as an extra barrier against the heat of my cup and my gloved hands, but there's no way that stain is coming out like this. Of course, Seth is wearing a super expensive, designer-brand workout shirt because nothing says *fall in love with me,* like ruining an eighty-dollar shirt with scalding hot chocolate. Though now, I have an excellent excuse to invite him back to my apartment.

"Oh, darn it all, Seth," I say. Aren't I wholesome? "I think I'm just making it worse with this napkin, but I have a killer stain remover back at my apartment. If you aren't busy, I can spray it on there and let it work its magic before that stain sets."

Glancing past my shoulder at something, he shakes his head and turns his attention back to me. "Uh, yeah, that sounds good."

"Great." I smile. "Let's get going then."

Seth's hand falls on the small of my back. I bite down the shiver threatening to terrorize my spine at how simple a touch it is, telling myself that all we're going to do is fight a stain together, but my libido isn't getting the message. She's ready for another round of Seth turning us into a puddle, even if my endo is still rearing its ugly head, and my heart is wary of growing closer to Aarons.

With him, it feels like I could shatter, even more than I did with Brady, more than I ever have. And that terrifies me. But if I don't do this—I'll lose everything I worked so hard for, so it's a risk I'll take.

Everything will go back to normal, anyway. I can weather this.

I have to.

## CHAPTER NINE
# Miracle on 34th Street
### SETH

**THIS PLACE IS BECOMING** my favorite song.

When my shoes hit the cobblestoned pavement, the staccato rhythm soothed away my anxiety over the unknown. None of this makes sense. I was convinced I was dreaming, but a day later, either my dream is playing the long game, or I owe Jenny an apology, and faeries are real.

And when Ellie blew powder on my face, and the ground swallowed me whole, she sent me to an alternate reality.

One where I never got hit by a truck, and Maddie looks at me like she's just as gone as I was when I first saw her.

And we live in a college town ripped right out of a Hallmark movie.

Huh. I don't know if a college, holiday, small-town romance has ever been attempted. Ellie's going for all the tropes with zero fucks to give if it makes sense, then. Cool. I can get behind all vibes, no plot, I guess.

With each long stride forward through town, Maddie's whimper became the melody that looped over and over in my mind.

I tried to push my body past its physical limits. But as I passed onto the main street at mile three, the limit never came.

It had been years since I had run like that. The strange memories that have plagued me ever since I woke up in bed with Maddie tell me it's because I'm training for the combine and the draft. And there's no telling how long or far I would have gone if a hot beverage and a gorgeous smile didn't assault me.

I pull my shirt away, trying to keep it from sticking and burning everything there further, but I'm pretty sure it's too late.

You don't see the seething pain mentioned in the coffee-spill meet cute too often, but I'll insist on its inclusion from now on because, hell, this hurts. And this isn't cute.

Luckily, Maddie's apartment isn't too far away, and I can strip it off and let my chest breathe for a second.

The bar below her apartment is where I first ran into her in this world. She was reading a textbook at the bar. This Seth saw her across the room and recognized the reading material as something he was supposed to study for a Humanities class he was failing. It turns out that Maddie was perusing the book for fun since she'd already aced Professor Scott Calvin's dreaded Humanities introduction class.

Professor Calvin is a hardass and doesn't care if failing means I can't play in the big bowl game that will bring lots of donations and free advertising to the school. It's a backbone I'd applaud where I've seen how annoying it is not to be the one getting the special treatment. But now that I can throw a ball well again—I'd rather just coast through like I used to.

Since I couldn't in this situation, I begged Maddie to tutor me. My heart patters recalling the small smiles and stern, unamused looks Maddie flashed my way during tutoring sessions. Or our first kiss when I reached over her head to grab a book. She turned in shock, and I glanced down and needed my lips to brush against hers more than anything. A relieved gasp escaped her when her back hit the bookshelf, like all the tension I held inside for our first ten sessions was also within her.

If this is part of Ellie's Romancelandia, it'd be safe to assume that my story revolved around a happily ever after with Maddie. However much I'd protest that with the actual Madeline Finch, tree farm working, tutoring, flannel-wearing Maddie is someone I know I could fall hard for. But with every step we trudge up her stairs, an unsettling feeling coils deep in my stomach.

This is the start of the story, and we're already sleeping together, and her best friend is freaking Connor because, apparently, I have to hate him in every reality. It'd be funny that he's the best friend if there weren't a detail I never had with Jenny. He's her roommate.

I've read enough roommates-to-lovers in my time to know that this is their story, and I'm just the friends-with-benefits dick she has at the beginning who will lose her when she realizes she's been in love with Connor all along. I'll fade into the background, maybe reappear around the third-act breakup to get punched in the face by Connor, or perhaps I'll disappear completely, and people will wonder if I'm getting my own book or not.

Those are my only two options.

"Earth to Seth Aarons, hello!"

I blink back the film glazing over my eyes, and Maddie, on her tiptoes, reaching for a bottle of something resting on the top of a stacked washer and dryer, comes into focus. "A little help, I can't—"

"I've got it." My fingers fall on her hip, and I tug her close to me. Her rosewater scent fries my circuits, and I slow my reach for the bottle, savoring her soft curves.

"Any day now, Aarons," she says in an agitated, breathless whisper.

"I'm sorry. Is this the bottle you want?"

"Mhm," she whimpers.

I pull the bottle down, resting it on the top of the washer. Maddie's breath slows, and the pull between us tightens in my chest. Like I can feel how badly she wants me right now. Brushing her hair over her shoulder, I bring my lips to the shell of her ear. "What do you really want, Maddie?"

"Connor might be home," she whispers.

I press my lips to her neck and relish the shiver that works down her exposed arms. Sure, Connor's the end game, but I might as well enjoy my time on the page. If only the Ice Queen version of Madeline Finch could see herself like this. This gone for *me*. She'd be horrified, and I'd revel in every fucking second of it.

"So be quiet. Tell me, do you want this?" My fingers trail across the exposed skin on her midriff, stopping near the button on the waistband of her jeans.

"Yes," she sighs.

"Good girl. Put your hands on the dryer."

A small gasp escapes Maddie's lips. She places her palms against the dryer. With one hand hooked around her thigh, I hold her close to me, using my other hand to unfasten the button on her jeans and slip it under the cotton waistband of her underwear.

My finger splits her seam, finding her swollen center, slick and ready for me already. Held enraptured by the pattern of her heavy breathing, I listen to her quiet whimpers and moans as I swirl and flick according to her needs.

Hell, I would do this every day to hear those sounds.

My other hand leaves her thigh, exploring the curves of her body before gripping one of her breasts. Maddie bucks against my hand, and I hold her tight, matching her rhythm.

"That's it, Maddie. Give in." I coax her as her hands drop from the dryer, gripping the edge of the washer—everything in her tenses to the point of climax. I bury my lips into the side of her neck, rubbing the pad of my thumb over her nipple before grabbing it again and giving her two of my fingers.

Her legs quiver against mine. "Ride my hand, Maddie."

I press my palm flat against her clit as I drag two fingers in and out. Her warmth sends me to the brink of losing conscious control of this situation. I want to strip her of everything and slam her against this machine, but Maddie needs a very careful balance of gentleness and teasing to come, and it'd hurt her if I gave in to the primal parts of me clawing their way to the surface.

Maddie's hips buck back and forth as she thrashes against my fingers.

"Just like that, good girl. Come for me, love, let go."

Finally, everything in her shudders with a spasm and a loud cry. Her shoulders heave as she uses the washer/dryer for stability, and I relish her little aftershocks, still tracing her pleasure with my finger.

Maddie pivots right into my chest, breathless and shaking. She grazes her teeth on her bottom lip, tilting her chin towards me, fluttering her eyes closed when the pad of my thumb brushes over her cheek.

I smirk, running my finger down her limp, plump lip, swollen from biting down on it to suffocate most of her cries.

With flush cheeks and mussed-up hair, she looks decimated in all the right ways.

And I did that.

"We... need to get your stain out," she says with a wavering voice.

"Then take my shirt off, Finch, you know how."

Her brows crease in an annoyed frown. "God, you're arrogant."

"Maybe, Buttercup. But you like it." I wink. "It's kind of hard to deny after what we just did."

"Maybe I got it all out of my system." She grabs my wrist and drops it from her face with a scowl. "Maybe I'm over fuck boys."

I arch my brow, flashing her a wicked, crooked grin. "A little hard to believe, but I'm nothing if not a gentleman." I step back on my heels, hands in the air in mock surrender. "I'll just be over here."

Pinching the shirt's collar, I tug it over my head in a slow, deliberate way that Kennedy used to make me do for Instagram videos. Videos she'd always cut before showing my face because, apparently, she wanted to keep some things private. I hated when she'd used my abs for likes, but I obliged her because I was a dumb bunny. But now, I'm thankful for the practice because when I peek up, making sure my muscles are taut and flexed, Maddie's staring at me slack-jawed. Her perfectly round cheeks burn bright red like glass ornament balls.

"Quit ogling, weirdo." I toss the shirt at her and cross my arms and ankles, leaning against the couch, running parallel to the laundry closet in Maddie's open-concept apartment.

"Then quit posing like a goddamn model!" She huffs, marching towards the kitchen and slinging my shirt over her shoulder.

I follow her the few feet, allowing myself to be the obedient puppy dog I'm close to becoming. Maddie turns on her heel, and I'm quick to slam the cocky mask on. She wags a finger in front of my arrogant facade. "Your presence in the kitchen is strictly forbidden."

My lips twitch. "That scared you can't control yourself?"

She smooths the shirt out on the island counter and douses it with the stain remover. "Yes, I'm worried I'll murder you with access to all these knives. Wouldn't look good on my resume."

"Aww, come on now. Whose name would you scream if you did a silly thing like that?"

"I'd have my dignity to keep me warm. It'd be fine," she says, grabbing a brush and scrubbing the stain. Her shoulders bunch to her ears with tension, like her mind and body are at war.

I cock my head to the side. I'm used to sparring with Maddie in my world, but this Seth doesn't get much lip from her, so this sudden agitation is a bit out of character.

Not that I mind it. It's almost comforting and makes driving her to the edge even more satisfying.

"Maddie."

"Hmm?"

"Can you look at me?"

"Can't. I'm busy saving your shirt. You know, this thing is impractical. I know how expensive these are, and I don't think there's much of a difference between them and a regular workout shirt."

"The company gave me a few to wear while I workout, so if I get photographed or filmed on campus, it's in the photo. I didn't buy them."

The scrubbing stops, and Maddie purses her lips. "Wait, so this was free?"

"Yeah."

"Why am I trying to get this out, then?"

"I enjoy watching you rub stuff out." I shrug.

She rolls her eyes, dropping the brush on the counter. "You're lucky you're not in the kitchen right now." She wipes her hair out of her face and picks up her gaze, meeting mine. A tiny sly smile cracks the corner of her mouth. "But if you enjoy watching me, come here."

I hesitate, taking stock of the steak knives. None seem to be within quick draw reach, and I pick up my lean off the couch and march over to the island.

Maddie meets me, standing in between my legs. Her finger trails over the spot where the hot chocolate scalded me. It's a little red now, but I think I avoided the worst of it.

"I'm sorry about this," she says. "Does it hurt?"

"Ended up being fine." I smile down at her.

"Oh, good. I'm glad." Her finger traces the dips and valleys of my abdomen, curling up and exploring my chest and the tattoos inked like a Van Gogh. With every swirl, she dips lower towards my Adonis V, and my eyes close at the touch.

"Maddie—what are you—" I manage, my pupils dilating and my breath heavy until Maddie's lips capture mine, and breath evades me. Her hand slips into my gym shorts, and warmth envelops my dick.

I shudder for half a second before a growl threatens to rip out of me in response to her touch.

*Mine. Mine. Mine.*

"Shit, Buttercup—"

She drags her teeth along my bottom lip. "If you enjoy watching me rub stuff out, it might as well be something fun," she whispers before finding my nipple with her tongue.

She pumps harder, and any hope I had of playing this cool flies away. She has me in the literal palm of her hand.

She continues kissing down my sternum until she reaches my shorts. Her finger hooks into my elastic band, and she pulls it down and kisses the tip of my erection before taking it in her mouth. The heat of her, seeing her with her eyelashes fluttering in front of me. It shatters something inside of me.

"Shit, Maddie, if you do that, I'm going to—"

*Worship you forever.*

The thought suffocates the warmth curling through my body. Alternate Reality Maddie or not, any Maddie is too dangerous to my system. My heart is liable to get attached, and I'm not the endgame. I have to remember that. I've been the guy in love that gets left behind too many times. The power shift needs to be fixed fast.

"What the fuck? Seriously, on the counter, guys? I have to eat there." A loud, harsh groan stops us both, saving me. Connor stands in the hallway with a scowl directed at us beneath thick-rimmed glasses.

Maddie pulls her hand and mouth away with a cute little "oops" and an accompanying giggle that plucks at the heartstrings of the caveman I bury deep down inside, begging to flip her over my shoulder and march her into her bedroom.

Connor's frown flattens as he stares at her, morphing from anger into something resembling disappointment.

He's in love with her already.

Jealousy incinerates any good feelings that gathered inside.

*Mine. Mine. Mine.*

Well, that's not alarming or problematic or anything.

"Sorry!" Maddie giggles again. "I was just—we were—"

"Yeah, while I'd love to hear what excuse you're trying to make, Mads, we're running late for class."

"Right! Class!" She wipes a hand across her lips, and I groan.

Clearing my throat, I say, "I'll walk her there if you want to get going. Maddie and I have to finish—"

"Buddy, you're not finishing anything." Connor shakes his head.

"He meant I need to finish getting the stain out of his shirt because I spilled my hot chocolate on it. But it's a lost cause anyway." She rolls her eyes and ruffles his hair, walking by. "Give me a few to change?"

"Yeah. Fine." Connor's shoulders collapse. His eyes follow her as she leaves the room.

"I'll be right back, Aarons. Don't let the abominable snowman intimidate you." She calls down the hall. "Or you can join me."

"Yeah, I'm the threat." He snorts, shaking his head and glaring back at me.

I smile without saying another word and walk towards the bedroom, uninterested in an awkward staring contest. He stops me on my way with a hard hand on the shoulder. "Hurt her, and I swear to god, I'll find a way to break both your arms."

"Relax, we're just having fun. No one's getting attached."

He shakes his head with a sigh, marching in the opposite direction and slamming his door.

"Boy, he's grumpy today." Maddie laughs, tossing some clothes aside.

"Yeah, I don't think he likes me much." I scratch at my head.

"Who does?" She snorts.

"Someone thought I was okay last night." I flash her a crooked grin, eyes roaming around her room. "Even if I missed her this morning."

Posters of Ireland from when Maddie studied abroad litter the white walls, and twinkling lights and vines hang through the room. Her desk is organized and warm; unlike mine, I get the sense that it's used for its intended purpose.

"Sorry." She flushes. "I had to study for a test, and I didn't trust you not to talk me out of it." She attempts to pull her shirt off, but her head gets stuck in the hole. "A little help."

I walk over and free her. She smiles, pressing a quick kiss to my lips and flashing an intoxicating smile. "I have to go," she says, grabbing another shirt and tossing it on.

Right.

I cup her face, greeting her mouth with a soft, toe-curling kiss. A faint whisper of hot chocolate wraps around my taste buds as my tongue plunders and explores. I don't know how much time I have before she falls for Connor, but I'm fucking addicted to her at this point. I pull away, smirking as she runs her fingers along her lips and furrows her brows in confusion.

There's some time left. I might as well enjoy it.

# CHAPTER TEN
# Frosty the Snowman
### MADDIE

"PLEASE DON'T PUSH the little children." My hoarse voice carries through the frosty air, falling over the ice pond. A ruddy-nosed man rolls his eyes, still skating aggressively, and weaving through the packs of unsteady children. I've had to ask impatient adults not to knock past the tiny tots far too many times over the past week.

It's frustrating. And the cold is biting. And most of the time, I don't understand why anyone would willingly live in a place where the air hurts your face.

But sometimes, I understand it even if I don't care to admit it.

Quiet times like these, when the stars seem to shine a little closer, maybe even a little brighter in the cloudless night sky. And a soft, fresh blanket of snow drifts to the ground.

White lights twinkle against the dark expanse, strung through the overgrown balsam fir trees that line the edge of the skating rink. In the distance, smoke from the wood fire burning in the main barn rises in the air, the smell of charred wood carrying on the wings of a subtle breeze, warming my lungs and soul, as I stand against the ice skates rental hut, clutching my third hot chocolate of the day.

This job is great for people-watching.

In general, I dislike people, sure, but I don't know. Something about this environment brings out the best in people.

There's a vulnerability involved with skating for the first time, and the couples attempting to skate together are my favorite. One of them wobbles like Bambi learning to walk, while the other is strong and supportive, flanking their side. Like they're telling their partner that even when they don't know what they're doing, and things look ugly, they've still got them.

They'll be there.

And there's something gorgeous about that.

I don't know if I'm capable of that kind of vulnerability, but I'm suddenly yearning to be a person who risks the fall.

With a smile, I hum along to the love song disguised as a holiday tune playing over the speakers wired to a few trees around the pond and wipe down a pair of rental skates just returned to the little hut. After a week of work, I've fallen into a comfortable routine here, walk to the back counter, wipe down and spray disinfectant on the skates, then pivot and put them in their allotted cubicle under the checkout counter, and grab a sip of hot chocolate.

Tonight's has a peppermint swirl because I'm adventurous like that.

With a final swipe of the cloth, I turn to put them away.

A small but imposing figure stands ready to pounce on the other side of the counter. A deadly, cutting glare narrowed on my face.

"Jesus, Jenny, stealth much?" I put my hand on my heart. "You startled me."

Her red-lacquered lips stay curved into a frown as she runs her fingers through her tousled curls.

I'm trying my best not to be envious of her silky tresses. This Maddie doesn't own any hot tools, and I'm too broke to remedy that. I've tried other heatless ways to tame my frizzy mane, but it's been no use. Part of this curse is apparently infinite bad hair days.

At least beanies are warm, so there's that.

"Can I help you?" I ask after a few more seconds of awkward staring.

It's weird seeing Jenny like this. I have some memories of her, so I'm not shocked, but having a memory and going through something yourself are two very different experiences. And Jenny standing here stuffed in a white fur coat with lash and hair extensions and a contoured face is bizarre.

My heart patters with a sense of longing. Ellie wasn't too creative with our backstory. It's the same, just reversed, probably trying to give me a taste of my own medicine.

I'd roll my eyes, but it's working because thinking of Jenny feeling this heartbroken just looking at someone who used to be her best friend fills the pit of my stomach with remorse.

When I was the baddie, I only thought about the sacrifice I needed to make to get what I wanted, but I never thought about how it made *her* feel.

It's like mourning the dead and seeing the corpse every day. Like a part of my soul was ripped out without my permission, I can see it, but I can never have it back.

It sucks.

"So what's the deal with you and Aarons?" she asks.

"Um—"

*Funny story, I'm in love with him, and I need him to fall in love with me, too, so I can have ten minutes of my life back in an alternate reality, which is the real world... I think. My grasp on what is real and what's not is a little fuzzy.*

No, I can't say that.

"I'm tutoring him?" I say, rubbing down the counter.

"Like at your apartment? Because Cali saw you two going there earlier this week, and she said his hand was on your back."

*Good thing Cali didn't see where it was once we were inside.*

My cheeks flush with heat, recalling his palm pressing on my clit as he drove two fingers into my entrance and stretched it wide, an ungodly feeling pooling between my thighs in response like he was casting a spell and claiming my soul with every pump.

Hell, I can't wait for this soulmate bond to stop being a thing.

Jenny drums her manicured fingers on the top of the pine counter. Her claws clack impatiently with every pass. Right. She asked me a question.

"I accidentally walked into him, spilled hot chocolate on his shirt, and offered to get it off. That's it." I swallow, clearing my throat and my head.

"Uh-huh, that's a cute excuse."

"It's the truth."

"Whatever, look. I just wanted to come here and tell you—because I still care about you—not to get too attached to him because I know how clingy you can get with people. Seth and I are getting back together soon, and I don't want to see you get hurt in the aftermath. Okay? God, you're still so cute." She leans over and scrunches her nose, booping mine with her finger.

"Thanks for the heads up." I drop my gaze to the rag in my hand. I don't read too much into part of Jenny's words. They're something I would say to get under someone's skin. But the part that terrifies me is the reality that Jenny is my competition. Jenny, with her perfect hair, flawless face, and wardrobe—there's no way I stand a chance against someone like her.

And if I don't get Seth to fall in love with me, then I'm just as screwed in the real world as I am here.

Well, fuck.

## CHAPTER ELEVEN
# Bad Santa
### MADDIE

IT IS a truth universally acknowledged that when a woman is in firm possession of a thousand finals papers to write, Seth Aarons's touch becomes more distracting than Santa Claus riding a unicycle while playing the kazoo.

Is that a terrible analogy? Maybe.

Is that unfortunate, considering I'm trying to finish a paper for my British Literature class? Probably.

Is Seth's hand burning a hole in the side of my thigh? Abso-freakin'lutely.

"I need to focus." I scold as his hand slides ever closer, flirting with the hem of my midi skater dress under the table in the library.

"What can't you focus like this?" He smirks, turning his page with his free hand.

"No, and you know it. Don't be cheeky."

It's been two weeks since Ellie transported me to Balsam Hill, and I'm still no less used to his touch's scorching sensations on my body. Another unfortunate fact, considering I only have two more weeks to make him fall in love with me, and all Seth seems keen on doing is dominating the fuck out of me with his fingers.

Okay, so not the worst-case scenario, but if I have any chance of getting those ten minutes back, I need him to start falling for something other than the way his name sounds coming off my lips when I'm orgasming.

Seth leans in. His breath falls hot against my neck as he brings his mouth to my ear. "I need another book for this paper. Want to come?" He pulls away, a pleased twinkle shimmering in the recesses of his gaze when he sees me shiver at his proximity.

My pulse skitters with anticipation.

This Seth Aarons may not be as clever as the other one, but he's clever enough to make an innuendo when he wants to

Lately, I've tried to space out our little... whatever these are... to help manage my flares a bit, making excuses for why I can't see him, or just avoiding responding to his texts until my libido can be trusted not to destroy us both. But even with those strategies, this whole thing has been hard for me. Sometimes it's like he's a piece of forbidden fruit that I know I shouldn't eat, but it's the most tempting goddamn thing. And I have caved a few times, answered his text, and gone over when I shouldn't have because I genuinely like fruit. Honestly, I know the pain isn't ideal, but a part of me wants to argue that I'd be in pain anyway. I should try to control what I can and enjoy the journey more.

Get my mind blown on the way for a change.

"God, you're the worst—but yes." I sigh, trying not to seem too eager as I bolt up out of my chair. "Yes, I want to come."

He snickers, his hand falling to my hip, and he walks me to the stacks.

I lean against the dusty, neglected shelves with a smile as he mirrors me across the way. He rakes a slow seductive gaze down my body with a smug grin.

"What?" I laugh after a few beats.

"Nothing. I just like looking at you."

My brow furrows. "Well, that's weird to say to me, Aarons. I don't think I look any different today." I frown, glancing at my clothes. "Another day, another flannel—you know, that's my motto."

He snorts. "Have I mentioned how much I love your flannels?" He reaches for me. His hand falls to my back under the flannel, pulling me against his chest. "I've always wanted to see you in one of mine, but this is almost as good."

"You don't—" I search his face. This Seth doesn't wear flannels. All the weird things that have caused me to pause over the past two weeks avalanche internally, like how he woke up from a dead sleep and seemed to be surprised to be in bed with me, even though he was the one hours earlier begging for my return. Or when I ran into him in town, and he said there was so much to look at. Oh, no. Oh shit.

No. No. No.

"Do you know?" I hiss.

"Know what?" He cocks his head to the side, kissing the nape of my neck.

"That I'm not—shit." I shiver as his lips brush against my skin. "That this isn't—I'm trying to—you know this isn't real, don't you?" I finally push out.

Seth pulls away, and his eyes widen. "Wait. Do you?"

"Be a weird thing to say if I didn't."

Seth studies my face, his lips twitching. He blinks. Once. Twice. And then a huge, mirthful laugh bleats out of his obnoxiously kissable mouth.

"What?" I throw my hands up in the air in exasperation.

"This whole time, I kept thinking, man, it'd be funny if Madeline Finch could see herself right now, and you're telling me, you, my Satanic Barbie, have actually been here?" He wipes away a few tears collecting under his eyes. "Oh, that's rich."

"It's not that funny." I scowl.

"Oh no, you're right. I see absolutely no humor in the fact that I've had you begging for me, thinking it was some docile fictional Maddie, but it's been you."

He steps forward. My back finds the bookshelves. His hands press to either side of my head. My body betrays me, screaming to lean and brush my lips against his. "You've been starved for me, Madeline. How has that felt?"

"Now that I know it's you, Lumberjack Frasier, I can confidently say I've lost my appetite." The words fall out of my mouth in an unconvincing wispy way.

Okay, I'm still a little hungry.

Maybe even famished.

God, I want to kiss this infuriating man.

"Maddie." He tsks, twisting a lock of my hair around his finger. "You and I both know I have you wrapped around my finger here and that I've been showing you mercy—maybe don't push it, or I'll be tempted to make you the lovesick puppy you've turned plenty of guys into over the years."

Anxiety roils in the pit of my stomach. I'm not proud, but I know if Seth wanted me at this point to be just about anything, I would comply.

"Maybe I don't want mercy." I slap his hand down from my face. "And maybe I think you're entirely too confident, Seth. You're not all that and a bag of chips."

"All that and a bag of chips." He snorts. "You're so wholesome. So cute…"

"Claws still work fine, bud." I wiggle my fingers in front of his face.

He catches my wrist, rubbing slow circles on the inside. I swallow, hoping he misses the erratic way my pulse skitters at his touch. "Ten minutes. You'd forget there was ever a Seth Aarons you hated and be begging me to kiss you in ten minutes."

"Set a timer. I'm free."

He cocks his head to the side. I don't think he expected me to accept his hypothetical challenge. "Your funeral."

"Boy, you're going to be so embarrassed when that timer goes off."

"Very cocky for someone I've had back arched, crying for me multiple times just this week."

"I know my heart and your personality will be enough to

repulse me," I say with all the confidence I severely lack. Seth awake in this world is the worst-case scenario when I'm trying to get him to fall in love with me. Especially when the woman he's actually in love with just told me she wants him back. I don't know what to do, but running away and hiding, however tempting, won't get Seth where I need him, so I have to try something.

"Want to make it interesting?" he asks, resting his forearm above my head with a devilish grin.

"What were you thinking?"

"Give me ten minutes. If you're not begging me to kiss you at the end, I give you permission to have Ellie write an hour of my life in whatever way you want, me in a chicken suit on the side of the street, me worshiping the ground you walk on...."

"Oh, you in a chicken suit worshiping the ground I walk on, tempting." I run my fingers together, all evil-like.

"They were two separate ideas...."

"My prize. My rules." I wag a finger in his face.

He rolls his eyes. "Whatever, you're not going to win anyway, so I'm not too worried. Now, when I win."

"You won't—"

He silences me with a determined stare. "I will, and when it happens, I get to write an hour of yours." His eyes swirl and sparkle with an alluring mischief. "And I won't be merciful for once."

With a large, doom-filled gulp, I consider my options. Opening myself up to this kind of vulnerability with the real Seth Aarons is a terrible idea. Seth's right, there's no way I win this, but it's the only way I can get close to him again. No way he'd kiss me for the sake of kissing me now, and if I want my deal with Ellie to come through, I will have to sacrifice my dignity a bit in this world for my real life.

As for the hour—I don't know how many interactions Seth has had with Ellie, but I'm not too worried. I doubt she'd rewrite a page for either of us over this silly bet.

"Aarons," I extend my hand out for a shake. "You have yourself a deal."

Seth grasps it, tugging me against his chest before cupping my face and walking me back against the library stack. "Well, this seems familiar...." I exhale.

"Except this time, you can kiss me like you wanted to."

"Yeah, I definitely didn't want to kiss you at the bookstore."

"Darling, I saw your face." His lips twitch. "You were looking at me like you are now, desperate for me to bury my mouth into your neck, maybe graze my teeth along your skin with a little bite," he says, in a low murmur, running one of his fingers delicately along the side of my neck.

Heat burns my cheeks as sparks follow the drag of his finger. We haven't even started yet, and I'm seconds from begging for a kiss, so that's cool. Definitely about to lose a fair amount of dignity here. "Have you set the alarm yet?" I ask in a strained voice.

"You sure you don't just want to wave the white flag now?" He smirks, sliding his phone out from his jean pocket and resting it on a shelf near my head. "Because there's no coming back from this, Madeline."

"Boy, you're so undeservedly cocky."

"We have the same memories from the past two weeks, right? Because I think my cockiness is pretty valid considering how many times I've had you begging for me already."

"You're wasting your time, Aarons."

"Baby, all I've ever needed was five minutes with you." He winks. His hand falls on my jawline, and his fingers brush the nape of my neck, tangling in with my frizzy locks. "I like your hair like this, you know?"

I scoff.

"I'm serious." His eyes soften. "It reminds me of the first time I saw you."

My eyebrows bunch together with confusion. That timeline is wildly inaccurate. "I'd already dyed my hair when you met me at

Tyler's party. Not that I know when we met or thought about it ever."

"Smooth." He snorts. "Met you, yes, but I saw you before that." He lowers his head, bringing his mouth millimeters from my jaw. I ache for his lips to press against my skin, but I'm met with hot air blown softly against it instead.

My breath hitches.

"Already going quiet on me?" He laughs.

"When—when did you—" I can't get the question out. He slips a hand under my flannel, over my bare shoulder, and peels it off, trailing a finger down my arm. His mouth meets my ear.

"You look good in these, but I think you'd look better in one of mine. Do you know how many times I've fantasized about that, Maddie? Or how wild you drove me that first year? How bad I wanted you the first time I saw you? The stomach aches you always elicited after. It's only fair that I return the favor. Darling, you can be the dope in love now."

If Seth's proximity and touch weren't frying my circuits, I might be able to process the fact that he's admitting that there was a time and place, however short, where Captain Pretentious harbored powerful feelings for pre-makeover Maddie. Or maybe I'd never be able to process that news bomb because what the actual fuck?

I try to open my mouth to say something, anything, but all that my voice box and lips manage without a functioning brain is "mmmphk-flannel-okay."

"That's really interesting." A warm chuckle vibrates Seth's chest, humming along to the heightened frequency my entire body is buzzing to. He brings his mouth to the shell of my ear, "Don't worry, Madeline, I'll show you the same mercy you've shown others when you're a goner."

"Ass." I try to hiss, but it comes out marred by heavy breaths. The tightness in my stomach is getting unbearable, and I need relief. I reach out to undo the button on his pants, but Seth grabs my hands with a tsk and pins them above my head.

His free hand moves up the side of my thigh, dancing under the hem of my dress. "Can I?" he asks.

With a whimper and a nod, I give him my consent.

At an agonizing glacial pace, Seth pulls down my fleece leggings and underwear, just enough, before slipping his fingers under the two layers, tracing the crook of my thigh, and touching me everywhere that isn't screaming in need right now.

With each graze of his fingers, embers spark along my nerve endings with anticipation until a slow-moving fire crackles under my skin, and flames lick my heart alive.

"Do you want my fingers, Maddie?" Seth asks, wearing an annoyingly smug smirk on his face.

"Yes, please." I fight down the "asshat" that wants to follow those two words. I have to go to class at some point today, and I'd rather not goad him into playing see-how-long-Madeline-Finch-can-last-before-she's-a-puddle-of-I-Love-Seth-Aarons-Goo.

Or worse, have him work me to the edge and close up shop.

"Such a good girl for me." He winks, finding my clit. I jolt when he circles it. I'm already embarrassingly ready for him, considering all he's done is blow air on my jaw and earlobe. But I can't help it. This whole soulmate shit sucks because Ellie made it so my body only responds to him, and with the frost inside him that probably grew three sizes today, he doesn't feel anything.

"Oh, you're so fucked." He chuckles. "Baby, why'd you even agree to this? Can't you feel how you call to me like this?"

Yes. Yes, I can, asshat.

"Say the words, and the torture ends."

He presses on my bud, reading my rhythm and matching my needs so that he brings me to the edge, and then he slows, never letting me fully get there. "Seth. Shit," I reach for him. I don't care that we're in a library. Nobody goes back here anyway. His lips pause inches from mine, and he dips to the corner of my mouth as my breath hitches.

"Say I won, Madeline."

I let out a whimper.

He brushes my hair over my shoulder, gazing at me like he's sympathizing with me in my current situation. I don't want his pity, even if I feel pitiful. "Don't fight this. Let me finish you. I want to hear you say my name again."

"You win, Seth," I whisper. "Fucking kiss me already."

Slowly, Seth pulls his fingers out and leans forward with a devilish set to his mouth, stopping an inch from mine. My chest heaves against his, my lips remain aggravatingly unkissed, and they demand satisfaction. Instead, with a smirk, Seth sinks to his knees, and a gasp escapes me.

"I might be too loud." I catch his shoulder, glancing around. We're in a secluded area, but if I've learned anything in the past two weeks, it's physically impossible for me to be quiet when Seth is involved.

"Do you want my mouth?"

My eyes close, and the pit in my stomach coils just thinking about him buried in my skirt. "Fuck, yes," I whisper.

"Cover your mouth then," he says. He picks up my skirt, and his breath falls hot against the inside of my thigh as he hooks my leg over his shoulder. "Fucking hell, you're beautiful."

If I thought I was Seth's before, it's nothing compared to whatever magical transference is happening here. He's not just buried underneath my skin anymore. He's in my bloodstream, curling his way from my heart to my toes and claiming every inch he passes through. I try to steady my breaths, try not to melt into the whimpering mess I'm close to becoming, but the minute his tongue lashes out against my bud, I'm a fucking goner.

"Seth, I need your fingers."

A satisfied growl rumbles, vibrating against my clit, and the growing tension makes me question if I need his fingers. I'm so fucking close to release.

But then a finger gently finds my entrance and flicks against my g-spot. I congratulate myself for doing something for myself, even if I'll regret the smug look on his face later, because god bless Seth Aarons's fingers, everyone.

Another lick. Another suck. Another pump of his fingers and I'm reduced to nothing more than a moaning, whimpering mess. My muscles tighten, and I writhe, my back arching, toes curling, and the fire that's been crackling along my nerve ends singes everything in an all-engulfing blaze.

Seth continues to explore my clit with his tongue as I spasm on the comedown, and I relish in the warmth of the aftershocks. If he's down there, I don't have to acknowledge what just happened or how significantly fucked I am.

Because I desperately want to do that about ten million more times before Christmas, but it's only Seth "Tragically More-Annoying Ross Geller" Aarons's tongue that seems to hold the magic key to my heart and... other areas.

"Fucking hell," I whisper, as eloquently as ever, wiping my hair out of my face.

Seth pulls up my tights and presses one last kiss on the outside before rising from below my skirt. His eyes sparkle with mischief when he meets my stare. Holding my attention arrested under his heated gaze, he lifts two fingers to his mouth, licking them clean.

An alarm blares to the right of my head, and I jump. Seth reaches for his phone. His tongue darts along his puffy lips, glistening in the low light. With a lean, he drags his teeth along the shell of my ear. "Victory's never tasted so sweet." His hot breath sends shivers down my spine, and his smirk grows deeper. "Don't worry, Madeline. I'll be gentle."

He pulls away, winking at my heaving chest, and saunters out of the stack before I'm able to respond. Hitting his hand on the top of the doorframe, he pauses. "Make sure you change before class. I don't want you catching anything going out in the cold soaking wet," he says without sparing me a second glance.

And I let myself collapse against the bookcase to catch my breath.

Well. Fuck.

# CHAPTER TWELVE
# The Nightmare Before Christmas
## MADDIE

"BE a good girl and retract the claws, Madeline."

The familiar words echo in a haze. I blink away the fog, and I'm back in the bookstore in the Romance section with Seth.

Again.

I don't remember coming here, though. The last thing I remember is falling asleep.

Something is off about how the bookshelves slant. Vertical bookshelves don't make sense, but I don't give too much thought to it because a man stands in front of me, threatening to devour me whole.

Seth's wearing his signature beanie and hideous flannel. His green eyes sparkle as his gaze rakes down my body, flames licking over every inch he travels. "I'm guessing you think I should kiss you, huh?"

I open my mouth, but nothing comes out, and his smug lips twitch.

He steps forward. "Already going quiet on me?"

I manage a simple nod of my head. There's no room for talking when my mouth has a one-track mind aching to brush against his.

With a bit of tenderness, Seth runs his thumb over the pad of my lip and lowers his head with a chuckle. "You're going to be so desperate for me in whatever world we're in, you know that, right? You're mine now, Madeline. I own you, and I'm going to enjoy destroying you. I've heard you're cute when you're in love, in any case. I bet it'll suit you better than Malibu Loki."

I whimper as if in agreement, and Seth captures my lips with his. It's a soft brush at first, but that tiny ember sparks alive into a greater blaze. Soon it's consuming me, burning away any piece that doesn't belong to Seth until I'm an unguarded molten heart and flesh. "I need you, please," I whisper against his lips.

"Of course you do. But do you think I'd fall for a pathetic worm like you? When I could have Jenny? You'll never be the endgame, no matter what you do or who you are. I'm just doing this to fuck around with you because it's amusing to see you like this. So why don't you beg for me some more, and I'll reward you."

My fingers tangle into the curls on the back of his head as the tiny, powerless "Yes sir" passes over my lips. He slides his hands down the front of my pants into my underwear.

"You see how you respond to me when I touch you, Madeline? You're never going to feel this way with anyone else."

He hurries his rhythm, bringing me toward the edge but never pushing me over. "And you know why, don't you? Do you remember how you felt the first time you saw me? How you've been lying to yourself ever since. Tell me, Madeline. Tell me now, what did you feel?"

I bite my lip, dragging my teeth in a slow, agonizing graze.

I still have some dignity to protect.

His circles slow, and he teases me, dipping to the crook of my thigh. "Say the words you've buried deep down. Let it out."

"I felt like my heart had never been whole, and it had found its other half, okay! But you didn't want me, so what does it matter?"

"Darling, I'll never want you, but don't you think it's time to be more honest with yourself?" He laughs and presses a kiss on my forehead. "You feel clammy. You doing okay?"

I dart up in bed, a cold sweat beading where Seth kissed my temple. My chest heaves as I try to gather my wits around me. "Fucking hell." I swipe my hair out of my face and check the time. It's four in the morning.

Great, because I didn't go to bed at midnight or anything.

There's a growing pressure in between my thighs that I can't ignore, and I slip my fingers under my waistband to provide myself with some relief.

The words, *I enjoy watching you rub stuff out*, play in my head as I come back down. *Seth*. Of course, this is what he did with the hour he won. A wet dream and masturbating to images of him. How original.

I grab my phone and clack out, "I'm going to kill you for that damn dream and the whole masturbating bit. You could have used that hour better, you know," and then fall back down on my pillow with a huff.

"YOU." My nostrils flare, marching into the gym where Seth is lifting a comically large dumbbell.

His biceps curl and the veins on his arms pop as he drags the weight forward.

"Oh hey, tutor girl, sleep well last night?" He smiles, not even deigning to look in my direction when he stands and gathers weight for the bench press. My eyes follow the thread of tattoos on his right arm, curling over his forearm, and pressure increases in the pit of my stomach. With a turn, he catches my stare, winking at my lack of discretion in this situation. I blush, and he flashes me one of his dimples, stretching his neck from side to side.

"Why do you insist on torturing me? What did I do to deserve this?" I cross my arms.

"Is that an actual question, Ms. Finch? Because I can have a list for you by the end of the year if you've somehow forgotten about your past."

I had. The more we stay in this world, the closer everything in our reality feels like a far less vivid dream than the one I had last night. Like it was someone else's life, and this is the real one.

"Fine. You win, Aarons. I'm fucked. Is that what you want to hear?" I toss my hands in the air.

"It does sound particularly sweet leaving those adorable lips of yours." He grunts out as he leans back to do a bench press. "Come on and spot me."

"What if I let this drop on you instead? That's a lot of trust."

"But then I couldn't reward you for being such a good sport tonight."

*Oh.*

My teeth drag across my bottom lip. "What, what would that entail, exactly?"

"Oh, that got your attention, huh?" He asks, pushing the bar up with ease. "Seriously, this is still too light?" he mutters.

"I mean, if it's a good reward, yeah. Maybe you need to let me decide if I'll like it."

Seth sits up, stretching his back muscles. "Judging by the library stacks, I think you'll like it just fine," he says, standing and walking me up against the wall. He glances around. The gym is empty beyond our two heaving chests. "Care for a preview?"

"I think it's only fair after the mean trick you played on me last night. I need some relief."

"You need some relief." He snorts, gathering closer. "My poor baby, let me take care of that for you."

My pulse drums against my ears with excitement. Seth's called me baby, sweetheart, darling, sure, but never *his* baby. Hopefully this is a step in the right direction.

"We have to be quick. The rest of the team is coming in

soon," he says, brushing a rash of kisses down the side of my neck, "But be a good girl and come to my house after practice, so I can take my time savoring you."

His invitation has an embarrassing effect on me, and when he reaches down there, he's going to know that too.

"Always so ready for me." He says, slipping a finger in. "Madeline?"

I mutter an incoherent response, eyes closed.

"Keep them open for me, baby. I want you to see who made you come so fast. I want you to know I'm doing this to you."

"God, I fucking hate you."

"No, you don't." He snorts.

"Your fingers are fine. It's your mouth that's the problem."

"You mean you aren't already worshipping it after the stacks?" He winks. "Ah. Well. I guess I'll have something to prove tonight, then."

"That sounds terrible. Maybe I shouldn't come—"

"Darling, you and I both know I control when you come. Isn't that right?"

I whimper as he brings me close to the edge.

"I get out of practice at seven."

"Okay." My muscles tighten, and I breathe through the heightening pressure. "Seven, I can be there at seven. Seven is good."

"You like seven?" He smirks, picking up his speed. It's so very inconvenient how good his fingers are. My toes curl, my back arches, and I crash along the other side with a greater force than whatever that pathetic excuse for an orgasm was this morning.

"I'll see you then, Buttercup." He kisses my cheek and helps me button my pants back up, running his hands through the sides of my hair and smoothing them down. "I'm going to be hungry. You want a pizza or something, maybe?"

"Pizza?" I heave against his chest. For all the times we've spent together the past two weeks, we've never eaten anything together. That seems more of a couple-y thing than whatever we are.

"Yeah, you know that round thing people sometimes get with sauce and cheese, usually put toppings on it."

"I like pizza." I nod.

His lips twitch. "Good to know where you stand on the Italian staple. Would you like to get some tonight?"

"Sure. Yeah. That sounds good." My eyes narrow to his lips, red and puffy, and any other thought flies out of my head.

"Sausage, green peppers, and onions, right?"

"Huh?" I watch his mouth move, aching to brush against them.

"You like sausage, green peppers, and onions on your pizza, right? Earth to Madeline, hello." He waves a hand in front of my face with a smug, satisfied smile. "Eyes up here."

"Oh, yeah. That is my favorite. How did you know?"

For a second, Seth regards me, almost bashfully, and rubs the back of his head. "Jenny may not be great at letting traditions go, so she still orders the pizza half-pineapple and ham, half-sausage, green peppers, and onions. Not a terrible combination."

"Oh." My heart squeezes thinking about Jenny going to our pizza parlor like we have every Friday since we were kids and ordering the same large New York-style pizza, and sitting there without me, and I have to fight back the tear threatening to trickle down. What kind of fucking monster was I that I did that to her?

"Hey—" Seth cups my cheek. "Madeline, I didn't mean to—it's okay."

"No, it's not, but thank you for going with her. I'm glad she had someone to lean on."

"Yeah, of course." He cocks his head, studying me, and then cups my face with his other hand, tilting my chin, so my lips meet his. He leans like he's about to brush against them—a real kiss, without a game to play.

But a loud shriek of, "Aarons, you son of a bitch! You're always early," interrupts us.

The room breaks into a raucous as an avalanche of football bros pour into the room.

And a smattering of "What's tutor girl doing here?" echoes off the weight machines.

Seth ignores the incoming crowd, his attention still pinned on me. "Seven? Okay, I'll see you then?"

I nod. He does this weird bro-ey handshake with a behemoth of a man, and I fall into the shadows and out the door.

## CHAPTER THIRTEEN
# Holiday Inn
### SETH

WELL, I'm fucked.

James spots me as I push the barbell toward the sky and breathe through the muscle fatigue. I'd much rather focus on my arms than what just happened or almost happened with Madeline, but my head won't quiet like it usually does when I'm at the gym. So instead, I'm lying here with my thoughts spinning in a tornado of panic. Over the past two weeks, I've had some glitching moments of weakness where I wanted to fall at Maddie's feet, but those glitches quieted the minute I realized Maddie wasn't just some fictional copy of someone I knew but *the* Satanic Barbie.

Today, though, something inside me cracked when she showed that maybe she still has a conscience, and a rush of feelings flooded my system.

I didn't just want to kiss her a few minutes ago.

I needed to. Like I was a man poisoned, and she was the antidote.

In our entire history, she's never felt like a life-saving device, just the death of me.

And I called her "my baby." Not only is that the douchiest

thing to call a woman—but I don't hate it? Not the term, but the thought that Maddie would want to be mine.

Because the truth is, I desperately want to be hers.

Again.

Fuck, I would have sold a kidney if she told me it'd make her happy the first time I saw her. But then she morphed into something I don't know. I could see the goodness in her, but then it went up in flames.

But that's the real Madeline Finch. She wouldn't be merciful if she thought I was a goner. So I can't give this Madeline Finch an ounce of compassion, either. It's survival of the fittest here in Balsam Hill.

"Dude, you can stop now, you know." James breaks into my train of thought as I struggle to push up the bar one last time. Yeah, I'm going to regret that in the morning.

"Sorry, I lost count. How many was that?"

"You did twenty-five reps. I thought we were doing heavy weights at fifteen today," he grunts, grabbing my bar and placing it back on the rack.

"Something on my mind." I shake my arms out at my side. The burn rushing through them is a sensation I'm growing addicted to again.

When the accident happened, I wanted to leave my old life behind, but these last few weeks have reminded me that I like some of this stuff. I like the strategy of picking the right play and reading the field. I enjoy counting through a workout and letting it quiet my mind. Maybe that's why my anxiety has been such shit since the accident because this was a coping skill I didn't even know I had.

I don't know. If I ever go back to the old Seth, I'll have to test that theory.

"Thinking about fingering fucking tutor girl again." James's lips tug into a sly smile. "She's a lot louder than I thought she'd be."

"I'll keep that in mind when she comes over later." I get off the bench, standing behind the bar.

"She's an odd choice when you could have Jenny back whenever you wanted, but okay."

Jenny. Fuck, it's terrible of me to admit, but I haven't thought about Jenny at all in the past two weeks. She's texted me a few times, but I'm not ready to face this version of her. It broke my heart enough to see her turning. I don't think I'd like to see the transformation complete. But she's probably my end game if Connor is Maddie's. Right?

Maybe I should text her back.

---

IN GENERAL, I am a well-spoken man. No matter how much shit Maddie has given me for being Captain Pretentious. If not verbally, then at least on paper, I write away the screaming thoughts swirling like a blizzard until they are a soft glide of a few lacey flakes.

But sometimes, even with all the words available, I have been speechless.

I can now say with complete and total confidence that Madeline Finch wearing one of my flannels in a pair of heels in my bedroom is one of those times.

"Do you like it?" She peeks at me. "I found it in the back of your closet, and I thought—"

"Baby, come here." I motion for her from across the room. This is the Maddie from my longest, hardest nights. "God, you've been such a good girl, you know that? Let me take care of you."

That phrase feels so douchey every time, but I love the pink blush that tinges on her cheeks whenever I utter it. So she has a praise kink? My ego can work with that.

Her teeth run over her bottom lip as she glances up at me, and

I see all the vulnerability in her gaze. "I have been on my best behavior, you know." She sidles up to me, threading her hand through my hair and pressing up on her toes. "So please play nice," she whispers, brushing her lips against mine.

There's a moment as the heat of her mouth captures mine where I feel us glitch, like old Maddie is kissing old Seth, and she's dominating the fuck out of him. I don't know, maybe it's the flannel and all my repressed underclassman fantasies coming true that pulls him out a bit, but she could tell me to get on my knees, and I'd beg for a taste of her.

And I can't let that happen.

I'm safe as long as she thinks I still have the upper hand.

The minute she catches on that I'm a goner, I'm screwed.

"Get on the bed, Madeline," I growl against her lips. "Now."

She whimpers, dragging her teeth across mine, and it takes superhuman strength not to beg her to let me worship her until the end of days. My knees buckle ever-so-slightly, and I hope she doesn't notice.

"I said, bed."

"Come with me." She tugs on my shirt, walking me forward, and I comply.

Doomed, Aarons. You are doomed.

I halt my steps and drop my forehead against hers. "Maddie," I whisper.

"Oh for fuck's sake, Aarons, would it be the end of the world if I knew you had feelings for me?" She lips.

It really would be because Madeline Finch doesn't show mercy.

With a slow tease of her fingers, Maddie undoes the first few buttons on her flannel, climbing onto the bed and exposing her black lace thong underneath. All the self-preservation safeguards I've built around my heart to keep this damn woman out go up in flames at that moment until they're nothing more than a mound of ashes, leaving my beating heart exposed for the taking.

"You know, you can be rewarded too." She beckons with a

crook of her finger, a little smirk I haven't seen in a while on her face like she knows she has me.

Like she knows she's always been my kryptonite, even when I've hated her guts, and she's proving to be the death of me yet again.

"So needy, all the time." I tsk, climbing over her. I won't give her the upper hand. I can't.

"You look pretty needy yourself." She nods to my pants, and damn it. I'm betrayed by one of the chief romance gods—grey sweatpants.

"It's cute you're concerned about me."

"It's cute you're about to not have balls." She smiles sweetly.

"That mouth, my goodness. I may have to teach you some manners."

"I look forward to being punished."

She sprawls out on the bed, looking like sin herself incarnate, and I take a second to steady myself. "You okay there, Aarons? You don't look so sure of yourself for someone who's supposed to know what he's doing. Maybe that dream set you up for failure."

Ah. A wide, wicked grin rakes across my face as I ready the ammunition I've wanted to shout at her since she marched into the gym. I'm glad I saved it because I need it to right the power dynamic.

"You know, funny story, Madeline Finch. I haven't used my hour yet."

Madeline's eyes widen in horror. "Wh—what?"

"So you." I boop her nose with my finger. "Had a wet dream about me on your own, sweetheart."

*They're frustrating, aren't they?*

"But you—" She squirms underneath me, the cogs in her head whirring like they're ready to explode. Heat grows on her cheeks, staining them a deep crimson red.

Hell, she's beautiful.

"And masturbated while thinking about me."

"No—I—you said—"

"And then texted me about it."

"But you apologized for it."

"Didn't correct you." I smile. "Was thinking about using it now. Make sure you have the best, soul-crushing, ecstasy-inducing sex of your life. But figured I could do that on my own just fine." I trail a finger up under her flannel, feeling her soft skin and relishing the goosebumps that pebble her arms with my touch. She's becoming an addiction.

I need to guard against this better. We aren't here for much longer, so I'm sure Connor will be swooping in and taking her from me any day now.

"Mmpphfkkk," she mutters, her eyes closed. "Fuck me."

"Mmmphfkkk fuck. We can work with that."

"Seth."

"Tell me what you want, Maddie. Whatever it is, I'll do it," I murmur against her skin.

"I want you."

I swallow the "you already have me" that threatens to burst out.

Fucked, Seth Aarons, you are fucked. She will go on a rampage on your head and heart when you both return.

But I can't get enough of her, like this, when it feels like she's vulnerable with me, even if it may be an act.

"Show me where you touched yourself when you thought about me. Put my hand there."

With a blush, she grabs my hand and slips my fingers under her underwear, and fuck me. She's already so ready.

I want to tell her I'm going to miss the feel of her, miss the way her body seems to call to me like this. And bury kisses into every inch of her skin, making sure she knows like this, when she appears unguarded and genuine, she's the most beautiful human I've ever seen.

I know. I know. I tell myself it's a sham. But no matter how many times I remind myself of that, there's still a huge, gnawing part of me that wonders, what if it's not? Because, like this, Madeline Finch is the girl of my fucking dreams. Like this, Madeline Finch has my heart in a death grip. Like this—I love her.

The thought terrorizes me, and I slip my hand back out. No, well, that won't do.

## CHAPTER FOURTEEN
# Home Alone
### MADDIE

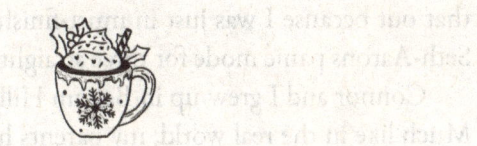

**THERE IS** something magical about a breath crystallizing in the frosty air. Carbon dioxide swirls into thin wispy clouds floating away into a cloudless sky, twinkling with winking chips of starlight. A reminder that no matter how dead I'm feeling inside, I'm still living, still breathing, and for today, that's enough. How many breaths have I taken for granted because I couldn't see them? How many days have I let pass without appreciating the little things that make the world so utterly fantastic? Focusing, rather, on future hypotheticals I thought would provide me with the happiness I've craved my entire life.

I don't know if it's this environment or if the humid concrete climate of Eastern Texas can supply me with this same satisfaction, but I'll slow down and enjoy it for now while I still can.

The balsam fir lining the edge of the frozen cranberry bog twinkle in the night, shimmering of the blankets of fresh snow forming a boundary around the rink.

I lean back on a wooden bench, my arms fatigued from shoveling new walking paths and clearing the ice before skating opened to the public today. A cramp stabs me in the abdomen, and I wince. No one is watching, so what does it matter if I react to this bullshit?

With a week before Christmas, the skating area is full of locals today since most of the college students have already left for home after a brutal Finals week. That week is a damn form of legal torture. How else could you explain the hold it had on me? So much so that I didn't question why I was putting myself through so much agony to study and finish things that didn't matter.

I could have failed. I could have let my work die and explored the town more, but I didn't even have a second to rationalize all that out because I was just in must-finish-all-the-work-and-bone-Seth-Aarons panic mode for three straight weeks.

Connor and I grew up in Balsam Hill, so we're already home. Much like in the real world, my parents have gone to some exotic location without me. Being the unfortunate, inevitable product of true love is the worst sometimes. It was great to see two people love each other growing up, but I don't know. It would have been nice to be a part of that, too. Is that selfish of me? Probably. But I'm a selfish person—they'd be the first to tell you that.

*We spend time with you every day. We need some alone time.* They'd say going off on vacations and leaving me with Jenny and her parents for every holiday, school vacation, and two or three dinners during the week where they'd go on dates.

*You need to be okay with being alone, Maddie. We can't give you attention all the time. Mamma needs attention from Daddy, too.*

It was awkward the first time I saw Jenny's parents interact with her. They told her she was the most important person in the world to them, and they loved her more than anything else in the universe.

I went home, eager to hear the same words. I told my mom I loved her more than anything else and asked if she loved me more than anything too.

*I love your daddy the most, but I love you second, pumpkin. Of course, I do.*

"Earth to Maddie. How have you not jumped me yet?" A low

laugh rumbles me out of a place I rarely travel to for obvious reasons.

I blink back a tear. A large, mittened hand comes into focus, extending a familiar sweater-clad to-go cup in my direction.

"Oh my god, I love you. Give me. Give me." I reach out for the sweet, hot vixen gripped in Connor's hand, and he smiles, pulling it away, beyond my reach.

"That's more like it."

I flex my fingers with my arms stretched, mimicking grabby hands. "Connor, you tease. Quit it."

"Oh, I'm sorry. I thought teasing was your thing." He has the audacity to wink at me, and I gasp.

"Not cool, bro. Take it back and give me my hot chocolate." I lunge forward, legs still sore from earlier, and slip on a patch of ice coating the grass. Connor tries to catch me, but he still has two hot chocolates in his hands and wobbles with me. "Save the hot chocolates! Don't worry about me!"

He widens his arms and steps back, and I tumble head-first into a bank of snow to a huge, mirthful chuckle. Ice falls down the back collar of my coat. I shiver through the freezing sensation terrorizing my spine as I shimmy it out. "This wouldn't have happened if you'd just given me the damn hot chocolate."

"Wow! Let's try that again, Mads. Thanks, Connor, for thinking of me and buying me my favorite hot beverage on your way to come to keep me company. You are better than any other person I know. How could I ever live without you?"

"I refuse to reinforce your ribbing with positive affirmations."

"Suit yourself." He shrugs, taking a sip of his drink and closing his eyes to savor it. "Fuck, this is good."

"I hate you." I plop back down on the bench and cross my arms in a pout. "I don't want a hot chocolate anyway. It's fine."

"That's too bad because Zach made it, so it has extra everything." He swirls it in front of my face with a teasing smile. Cocoa beans wrap a delicate hand around me, and my tastebuds water.

"Oh, god, okay, I still love you. You're the best." I reach, brushing against his mittened hand to grab the hot cocoa.

"Glad you're still easy." He smirks. The twinkling lights on the trees reflect off his glasses. First order of business when I get back to my old life is to do Connor a solid and tell him to get a pair of glasses because he's even sexier like this.

Do I want him back as my boyfriend, though? Unfortunately, no, I don't think so. Life would be so much easier if I did, but after living with him for three weeks, and watching him walk around in a towel, abs out for all to see. I know two things. One, Connor is an incredibly attractive man. And two, that fact does absolutely nothing for me. No butterflies. No sparks. Just an admiration and all my platonic love.

So what would I do with my ten minutes now? Getting the crown seems so hollow. After everything, I think it'd just feel like a symbol of all the shitty things I did to get to that point, and not a moment where I finally knew my worth like I wanted it to be.

Not that any of that matters when I'm nowhere near getting Seth to fall for me. I know, because he ghosted me this entire week. At first, it annoyed me because I had a goal to accomplish, but as the week spanned on, all I did was miss the damn man.

I'm attached.

How wretchedly inconvenient.

The bench creaks as Connor sits beside me, sipping his hot chocolate. I savor the warmth sliding down my throat, and the bit of cold cream I catch on the first drag.

"How's date night going?" he asks.

Every Friday from eight to ten, Pining All the Way's skating rink becomes *the* date place in Balsam Hill. Up to New Year's, we'll play romantic songs with a Christmas lilt to them and then change to sheer romantic ballads through Valentine's day.

Spiked hot chocolate from Cup of Cheer is for sale on a first-come, first-served basis, but it usually runs out in the first hour, and they discourage employees from partaking for obvious reasons.

My shift ended a half hour ago, so I'm just here to people-watch with Connor after a stressful week.

We fake-clink our cups of hot cocoa together. "It's going pretty well," I hum, glancing at my phone. Nothing. Still being ghosted by Seth Aarons, then, cool, cool.

I could have sworn we were getting somewhere at the gym, but he freaked out in his bedroom a week ago, and I haven't talked to him since.

A sharp spasming cough grips Connor next to me.

"Are you okay?" I ask as he continues to choke on his hot chocolate.

"Fine. Just went down the wrong way." He springs up from the bench and blocks my view of the pond. "You know what? I'm not really feeling into skating tonight. Maybe we should go home. Now. And watch a Netflix movie or something."

"Why are you being weirder than normal?" I ask with a judgmental raise of my brow.

"I'm not being weird. I'm just tired. Beat after finals, you know?" He rubs the back of his head, pushing his beanie off.

A familiar laugh and a breathy "Seth" send my heart into a free-for-all. He wouldn't do something that cruel. He knows I work here.

"How are you so bad at this?" A deep chuckle stabs me right in my unguarded chest. Apparently, he would.

"Connor, move," I order, standing on shaky legs.

Reluctantly, he shifts out of the way, revealing Seth skating around a far too wobbly Jenny Farrow, considering she glided with complete grace just a few days ago. She turns around, and he laces his hands around her waist, pulling her into him and flashing one of his huge, panty-dropping smiles.

Bitterness lodges in a ball in my throat, and I try to wash it away with my sweet and salty drink to no avail.

"Unclench, tiger, he's not worth the dentist bill," Connor whispers.

Relaxing my jaw, I take a few calming breaths, dragging the

frigid New England air through my lungs, but the hardening in the pit of my stomach won't soften, no matter how much I don't want this to bother me.

I knew this was the ending. I knew watching him fall in love with someone else was inevitable. And yet...

When he almost kissed me, I was hopeful. I could feel him, and he wanted me—*me*, not a moan, not a stroke of his ego. We were getting somewhere.

I could have sworn something cracked that day, but—a sharp pain grips my side, and I press in on it. "Shit," I whisper.

Connor rubs small circles on my back. I can sense Seth's eyes narrow in on us before I see them for myself. When I pick up my gaze, his stare's pinned to Connor's hand, a pinched expression hardening his face when all he's been is jovial and unaffected the past three weeks.

Huh.

Maybe the bond isn't as one-sided as I thought, then.

Only one way to find out.

I plop back down on the bench, kicking off my shoes, and lacing up my skates.

"What are you doing? Don't you want to leave?" Connor asks, hovering over me.

"I need you to flirt with me."

He snorts, crossing his arms in front of him. "Have you been sneaking the spiked hot chocolate?"

"No. But I'm close to breaking that rule." My fingers pull the laces up tight. "This is a good idea. Please."

With a sigh, he clutches his beanie with his hands. "I don't know, Maddie. Why do you even need me to do this?"

My eyes flicker to where Seth and Jenny are on the pond, and Connor follows the path of my gaze.

"You want to make the asshole jealous," he says with a frown.

"If I say yes, will you lose all respect for me?"

"Already happened when this whole thing started, don't worry."

"Oh, phew. Then yes."

Connor considers me for half a second before shaking his head. "Won't work with me. He's too full of himself to think I'm a threat."

My muscle on my right-side twinges, and I pull myself up from tying my skates, my body not appreciating being in the crunched position for that long. My eyes connect with Seth's, staring at me with an unfiltered attention, embers flicker along my skin just from his brief gaze.

"I don't know about that." I laugh, gesturing to the intensity of Seth's stare.

"Fuck, he's dumb." Connor drops on the bench and pulls his boots off. With his mittens in his mouth, he grumbles as his fingers fumble with the strings on his skates before sighing and looking at me. "I'll do it. But you owe me."

"Name your price."

"Dishes and trash for a week," he says, standing and extending his hand to help me.

"Deal." I accept his and walk to the edge of the pond, gliding along with ease as our skates hit the ice. "Where should we do it?"

Connor keeps hold of my hand, spinning me back around him. With a coy smile and an intensity narrowed on my face that I don't remember my ex-boyfriend ever possessing, he locks his gaze with me. He tries to run his hand through my hair, but it's mittened. His mouth twitches. "Mitten brushing isn't as sexy."

A giggle bubbles out of me. "Are you kidding me? Scratchy wool is hot. Like, I'm so freaking turned on right now."

"Yeah, okay." He rolls his eyes, wrapping his arm around my waist and pressing me close. "He doesn't deserve you, Maddie."

His breath tickles the hairs on the nape of my neck. I furrow my brow at the shiver he elicits. Connor's never managed that type of sensation before. I'm not used to having any feelings, and now they're all a jumbled mess.

But I know deep down, it's the words, and not Connor himself, that are having an effect on me.

They're nice. For the first time, it feels like someone values me. Maddie.

My eyes water, and I glance up at him. "Thank you," I whisper. "I needed to hear that."

"Of course, anytime. Want to get out of here?"

I nod. I don't need to know if the soulmate bond has thawed. What does it matter? Either it has, and Seth hated Madeline Finch so much that he can't get past that part of me. Or I failed, and nothing will melt it at this point.

Either way, I no longer need to be here and torture my heart. I can be at home with my best friend instead, put it on my lap to keep me nice and warm, and Connor will be there too.

God, I miss my heating pad because this pain is shit.

We go to slide off the ice, and something tugs at my elbow. I swivel, making eye contact with a pair of green eyes filled to the brim with warring emotions.

Anxious. Jealous. Forlorn, almost.

He clears his throat but doesn't say anything.

"Oh, hey, Connor. Look. Seth is here. Did you know? I hadn't even noticed."

"No shit." Connor snorts behind me. "He is?"

"You know, Seth. I was concerned that something terrible had happened to you after you didn't respond to my texts this week, so it's great to see you're alive and well." I pat his arm. "But I've got to go. We've got a pizza and a movie waiting for us at home."

"Madeline, can we talk?" Seth reaches again for me, and I try not to let the pang of sympathy I feel when I see his hand shake soften me.

"Madeline?" Connor chuckles. "God, you suck. Let's go, Mads."

I nod, narrowing in on Seth's hands and furrowing a brow. "Um. I think it's time I go home. Go back to your date, and we can talk later." I try to force a smile and not let on how everything inside feels like it's wilting. Whatever game we've been playing, I'm done. I lose. That's the inconvenient truth.

I love this man.

I always have.

All the things I thought annoyed me about him—his flannels, his wit, his damn smirk.

Your honor, I love them.

Really. Truly. Unfortunately.

Hate was just a lie I told myself to safeguard against what appears now was always inevitable. Me, standing in front of Seth, unguarded and vulnerable, and him only interested in me in a way that inflates his ego, only wanting to talk when his perceived property is threatened.

Suddenly, everything grips my pelvic area hostage, and it takes all that I have not to crunch and hug my midsection.

"Shit. Maddie, please, I fucked up but let me—" He tries to hook his hand around the crook of my elbow, but Connor slaps it down.

"You bet your ass you fucked up, buddy. Now leave her alone."

"I'm sorry. Are you part of this?" Seth stares down the slope of his nose.

Connor tries to return Seth's stare with a menacing glare, but he's still a golden retriever. "More than you are."

"Both of you. Enough." I snap. "There's nothing between us to fuck up, so don't worry about it. I get it. Promise. I'm not worth the hassle, and I deserve this. But I, I can't tonight. I'm sorry." I brush past Seth, turning my attention to Connor. "And you were right. I'm tired." I rub my arms in the frosty night air. I give up. What's the point of having ten minutes anymore? I'll love Seth like I always have, and he'll fall for Jenny. I deserve this. "I'm going home. You should stay and have fun, though. Maybe someone here will catch your eye." I plaster on a tentative smile and hide my pain. I'm so tired of being vulnerable. I'd rather go home and drag myself through the hell that's about to come alone.

Like I always have.

Because I'm good at being alone.
Promise.

## CHAPTER FIFTEEN
# Just Friends
### SETH

**MADDIE IS IN PAIN.** Panic tugs on my gut as Maddie glides away from the pond and unties her skates.

"You aren't going to follow her?" I ask Connor. It comes out strained as a growing pressure sits heavy on my chest.

This is the part of the story where I should get whacked in the face, and after seeing Maddie's shoulders slump and her skate away in defeat, I deserve it.

When Jenny suggested coming to the tree farm for skating, I knew what she was doing. She wanted to send Maddie a message. And I thought I'd be okay with letting it happen because it'd probably expedite Connor and Maddie's storyline before I fell harder for that damn woman.

And maybe, skating with Jenny would take my attention off the hungry flames that consumed me whenever I was in Maddie's orbit.

It was worth a try anyway.

But when my skates hit the ice and Jenny wobbled rather cartoonishly, I only felt panic.

*Maddie's in pain.* The thought froze me in the middle of the cranberry bog as I searched for her until my gaze fell on her angelic blonde hair tucked under a lilac beanie with a pom-pom on top. Connor's hand rested on her back, and a war of feelings stirred inside. Grateful that he was comforting her when I couldn't be the one to do it and jealous it wasn't me. Even if it was my whole damn fault to begin with.

And then it happened again, and I couldn't stand there anymore. I had to be close to her, or else I would shut down and have a panic attack on the ice. That's the only thing that made sense to me.

Jenny wasn't pleased with my sudden change in plans, but I doubt she would have suffered my antics well if I just sat on the ice, so I'll be the ass in every story.

And now, I'm standing here with a deep sense of dread and a gut screaming at me that Maddie doesn't feel well, and I need to do something about it.

"She said she wanted to be left alone." He shrugs, raising his eyes to meet mine with a cutting glare. "Which I suggest we both honor."

"But she's having a flare, and it's getting to be too much." I can sense it deep in my bones, like our molecules have somehow rearranged to become one and everything she feels is now ingrained in my soul.

Connor's eyebrows squish together, and he shoves his hands in his pockets. "Look, I don't know how much she's told you, but Maddie's a big girl. She can take care of herself."

I don't get it. If Connor's supposed to be Maddie's happily ever after, shouldn't he be the guy driven out of his mind wanting to take care of her? Shouldn't he be the one with shaking hands because he's overwhelmed with the need to run and scoop her up, bury her in a blanket and get her an unlimited supply of tea?

The tightening in my chest refuses to lighten as the frosty night air buries deep inside my lungs and freezes them shut. Slowly, I inhale, trying to draw in a single breath and steady my hands, but it's no use. Every time I think I find some peace, another sharp dose of anxiety holds me hostage, and I have to start over again.

"Hey, buddy, you okay?" Connor cocks his head to the side. Spots dot along the outside of his head. Oh no. That's my vision. "You don't look so good."

"Maddie," I manage before I wobble into Connor's arms.

"I don't think you're who she had in mind for me to meet when she told me to stay, but okay. I guess you're pretty enough." He grunts, righting my stance. "Let's get you off the ice and sitting before you crush someone."

No, there's no time to sit. "I need to find her," I say with a breathless delivery. Gathering whatever strength I have left, I unlatch my arm from Connor's shoulder and skate on my own. "Look," I say, facing him. "Jenny's at the other end of the rink. She's already pissed I bailed on her to come to talk to Maddie, but I was her ride here. Would you mind bringing her home when she's ready?"

"You want me to drive Jenny Farrow back to Greek Row on date night?" Connor's voice squeaks, and I imagine a blush growing underneath his rosy, frosted cheeks.

A wide smile spreads across my face.

I was so wrong about...everything.

If Jenny was right about the whole faeries existing thing, it only makes sense that she was right about soulmates too. My panicked, tight chest is evidence enough that she was right about Maddie being mine, so of course, Connor is hers.

"You'll be fine, bud." I grip his shoulder. "She doesn't bite much." My lips twitch as I skate away, calling for Maddie, but she's already in her car when I find her, and I get the urge to go somewhere first before her apartment.

**THE BELL PERCHED** above the door chimes as I enter the dusty bookstore with a sigh of relief. I've only tried to visit the store once since we've been sent here, but the door was locked that time, and I've been too busy getting ready for my bowl game and "studying" to try again.

"Ellie? Hello?" I call, shuffling to the counter. The drag of my feet echoes in the store.

The roll of a chair gliding across the wooden floor rumbles from the back room. "Oh, here he is, Chia. I told you he would come today. Figured out he has a soulmate and wants to make her feel better." She sings, dancing her way to the counter. The tabby Bengal weaves through her feet and rubs against her shin as they approach.

If this lady hadn't already cut my hair, blew powder in my face, and then sent me down a hole to an alternate universe, I might be concerned by her behavior, but now, well, any action is fair game in this bookstore, I guess.

"Come to use your hour, I assume?" She smirks, pulling a pencil out from behind her head. Long blonde hair falls past her shoulders, and the transformation around her glowing face startles me. Her cat eyes flicker to my face. "Oh darn, I took the glamour down, didn't I? Never mind, yes, I'm charming. Your hour, boy, focus."

"Right." I clear my throat. "Um." Panic seizes my chest, and I bury it back down. Maddie needs me. I can do this. "Can you stop her flare?"

Ellie's lips flatten, and her shimmer fades. "No, child, unfortunately, I can't."

"Oh." I rake my fingernails through the clipped hair on the back of my head. I only had one plan when I came here, and now I'm at a loss.

"But I can ensure she's comfortable and happy for the next hour if you'd like to use it that way."

"Sure, whatever will take the edge off everything, please, do that." I flex my hand at my side, working out the tremor.

"Soulmate bond is getting stronger with you two, I see." She smirks, motioning to my hand. "That's good. You both needed to learn that love doesn't come attached to some status you gain, like your quarterback status or her Greek whatever. But I'm worried about her, she needed to learn to love herself too before you both go back at Christmas, and I don't know if she's going to get there at this rate."

What Ellie is saying makes zero sense to me. Madeline Finch is the most self-confident human I have ever met. If anything, she should have had to learn to love herself less.

"I'm sorry, are we talking about the same person? Because I didn't think it was possible for Madeline Finch to love herself more."

Ellie clicks her tongue with a shake of her head. "We all wear masks when we're scared. Hers happens to be a very well-crafted one. Not saying it's right. Oh no, she was a piece. Just saying she may be more fragile than she lets on."

The hurt that hung in Maddie's eyes tonight suddenly makes more sense. In the chaos of the panic flushing over me, I figured it was just because she was in pain, and she was. But it wasn't just the physical kind.

"You'll have to grovel a bit, but you'll make it right, never you mind. Just take this cookie dough,"—she plops a yellow tube of chocolate chip goodness in my hand—where the hell did that come from? "And I'll send you on your way to right the ship."

"Thank you?" I blink as she blows a bit of dust from her hand into my face, and I'm suddenly falling into another black hole.

The words "Don't fart in the hole. Faeries live down there" echo in the void.

And I manage a frustrated "Seriously? I could have walked" before my mind goes blank.

## CHAPTER SIXTEEN
# Die Hard
### MADDIE

**I HATE EVERYTHING,** and everything hurts.

My back. My ovaries. A random spot under my ribs and neck. My uterus. My heart.

I barely got to the bathroom as the cramps intensified before I found myself with my head in the toilet, losing the pills I had just tried to swallow.

Oh, it's going to be one of those days, then. The kind where I writhe on the bathroom floor and beg for mercy until my body is so exhausted I fall asleep. Cool, cool, cool. At least my heart will be distracted.

I hug my heating pad tight to my midsection and let the cool tile relax me just a fraction.

I don't know what it is because on any good day, I don't yearn to go face-first onto the bathroom floor, but you add that pain and nausea in, and that tile is suddenly a freaking oasis.

The spasms hold my pelvic floor hostage. With a groan, I crunch into the fetal position and push the heat in, hoping it'll ease it. My skin grows hot with the heightened warmth, but I don't care, so I'll burn my skin a little. It's the only chance I have of getting this under control.

At some point, sleep finds me, and I blink my eyes open at a loud rap on our door. Did Connor forget his keys? Peeling myself off the floor, I make my best not-in-an-agonizing-amount-of-pain impression, straighten my shoulders, and shuffle to the door. This Connor knows about my disease, and this Maddie is a little more open about letting others see her at her most vulnerable. But in reality, Jenny Farrow is the only one who knows for a reason, and right now, I don't feel up for another life lesson. I want to survive the next few hours. That's it.

Without checking who's on the other side, I swing the door open and regret my extreme lack of caution.

Black ink swirls on his exposed, toned forearms, making a rare appearance because he's pushed up the sleeves to his Fezziwig University crewneck sweater. I can't look at his arms, then. I pull my gaze up. Auburn and chestnut curls peek out under a backward baseball cap as green eyes that usually sparkle halt my traveling stare. He has the gall to stand here, after everything, and look remorseful. Downtrodden, even. His face is pale, his lips parted, trying to catch a breath, and that tremor from earlier is still working its way through his right hand.

Am I the one sick here? Or...

"What are you doing here?" I blink.

"I need to take care of you." He exhales.

I can't help but read into his choice of words. He could have easily said, *I came to take care of you.* Or *I wanted to check up on you.* Or something like that, but I don't think people usually say they *need* to take care of someone.

"Well, I don't need any help, so thank you for stopping by, but—" I go to swing the door shut, and Seth's palm lands flat against the door, preventing me from closing it.

"Maddie, please don't shut me out. Not right now," Seth rasps. Like his breathing is strained, and he was the one who was tortured today, not the other way around.

A tear threatens to roll down my cheek, and I catch Seth's hand twitching at his side. "I was vulnerable with you," I whisper.

"And you threw it back in my face. Seth, that's not an easy thing for me."

"I know. I messed up big time, Buttercup. I'm so so so sorry. And I swear I will grovel at your feet for all eternity, wear a chicken suit and worship the ground you walk on, let you dominate the fuck out of me for every second of every day. I don't care. But please, for the love of god, let me take care of you right now."

"I don't know what you're talking about. I'm totally fine," I grit out while a pain grips my side, and I fight a crunch. My mask, thankfully, stays in place in one of my finer performances.

"Madeline Finch." Seth's voice drops into the low, stern cadence I've not yet heard outside the bedroom.

Don't think about the bedroom right now. That hurts too.

"You are not fine. I can feel you."

My pulse hammers in my ears. He can *feel* me?

"I'm—I'm sorry. What?" I blink.

"Something about this world." He gestures around. "Whenever you're in pain, I get anxious."

"Oh, well, that must suck for you, then." I force a laugh through another stabbing pain and step aside so Seth can enter the apartment. I don't have the will to fight, and after I worked so hard to get the last pill down to no avail, as stubborn as I want to be, if he *needs* to take care of me, well, I guess that wouldn't be the worst thing in the world. "But please don't worry, it's nothing, just my—" I bite my lower lip, debating if I want to be this vulnerable with him. Yeah, he was an asshole today, but he looks awfully remorseful, and he just said he'd wear a chicken suit for me, so...

"It's your endo, I know." He smiles softly, grabbing the crook of my elbow and guiding me toward the couch.

"I need to grab my pills in the kitchen first." I move away from the sofa. "How do you know about my endo?" I ask before the obvious answer lightbulbs its way into my brain. "Oh, damn it, Jenny."

"It's not her fault." He shakes his head. "Do you remember

sophomore year when you passed out and ended up at the nurse's office?"

"What time?" I snort, opening the fridge and groaning when I remember I have to bend for the water pitcher. A gentle push on my shoulder nudges me out of the way, and Seth peers in and grabs it. No verbal cues are necessary.

"Oh. Um. Didn't know there was more than one, but fair." He chuckles, reaching up for a glass and pouring my water. "This time you were walking home from class, and it was raining out."

"And some mysterious person caught me." I supply the end of that story.

"Yeah, I was the someone. And I kind of pestered Jenny to make sure you were okay." He has the audacity to plaster the cutest blush on his face when he hands me my cup, and any feelings of frustration I have for him melt away.

Freaking jerk.

"Seth Aarons." I smirk, letting my fingers brush against his on the exchange. "Were you worried about Madeline Finch?"

"Yes." He exhales, pinning the emerald in his eyes on me. "I've always worried about you, Maddie, even when I didn't want to. Why do you think I showed up at your house the night before all this happened?"

"Awfully weird of you to ghost and shatter me, then," I say, taking my pill and washing it down with water. After my last trip in the bathroom, I'm more hopeful about it staying down this time but then my right ovary twists, my heartbeat hammers at a dangerous pace, and suddenly I'm not so sure.

"I will grovel until the end of time for that, Buttercup, but let's get you to the couch first." He leans in and presses a kiss on my forehead.

I waffle again at the idea of him taking care of me. I'm still wicked anxious about opening up to him, even if he already knows most of the truth.

"That's an order, Madeline Finch," he says, dipping into his stern voice again. A muscle in his jaw ticks. "Please let me spoil you. Don't deny me that."

"So bossy." I click my tongue and shake my head. Hoping to wipe away the illicit images his bossy tone and fiery stare inspire. "You know, it's not as endearing when we're not in the bedroom."

"Oh, bullshit, you like me like this any time, sweetheart." He winks. "You. Couch. Now."

My gaze falls on his bossy mouth, and I graze my teeth along my lower lip.

"I'll kiss you once you're there. Stop looking at me like that."

"Oh, like what?" I widen my eyes and flutter my lashes. If Seth is struggling not to kiss me right now, I will torture him over it. Fair is fair.

"Fucking temptress." He growls, leaning down and brushing his lips against mine.

It's a tender kiss, apologetic even. Our first real one. He tilts his head, and I grant him better access, teasing the seam of his lips with my tongue and coaxing him out of his gentle possession of my mouth. The tug in my stomach toward him heightens as we explore each other like we're both finally accepting the bond, and now it's firmly stamped in place.

A sharp jolt grips me, but I don't want to stop. I never want his lips to leave mine ever again.

"Maddie." He pulls away, resting his head on my forehead. "Please go sit on the couch and let me get you cozy. I'll make you a hot chocolate. We can snuggle. You can fall asleep on me. How does that sound?"

"Pretty fucking fantastic." My chest heaves against his. And it's not a lie. It sounds like an absolute dream. Maybe being vulnerable wouldn't be the worst thing in the world if this is the result.

Seth guides me to the couch, and I lower myself down, gathering the heating pad I keep there at all times and cuddling into it. Grabbing a blanket from the top of the couch, he wraps me up like I'm the snuggest burrito, tucking it around my back and making sure not an inch of skin is exposed to the cold air in the apartment.

"Do you need anything else before I put the cookies in the oven?" he asks.

"Just your unconditional love and maybe some fuzzy socks."

Oh. My medicine probably hasn't kicked in yet, so already having verbal diarrhea isn't a great sign for me. Being vulnerable is addicting.

He chuckles. "Already getting needy."

My heart plummets into the ugly depths of my chest. Damn it, see, this is why we aren't vulnerable with people, because no one wants to see my soft side. It's repulsive. "I'm sorry, I –"

"I mean, unconditional love I can do, but fuzzy socks? Asking a bit much." His lips twitch. I toss a pillow at his obnoxiously attractive head. But he's unfortunately athletic and shit and dodges it. "Where are they, love?" He dips his head, brushing my hair out of my face, and presses a kiss on my temple.

"Top drawer. Mind the lingerie. That was for a night that you ghosted me, and I need to return it."

"Oh, that's a dirty play." He rubs his hands to his heart like he's been wounded, walking into my bedroom.

I smirk when I hear a tiny "Oh, fuck."

I picked out a particularly spicy red lace number last week that made me look like a present that needed to be unwrapped.

"Have I mentioned how sorry I am?" He bellows.

"Once or twice," I holler back. "Just bring me some socks, and all will be forgiven until the next time you leave."

He pushes his sleeves past his elbow before kneeling beside the couch and gesturing for my feet. "I'm not going anywhere, so unless you have running plans of your own, I think you're stuck with me, Madeline."

"Why would I run when you bring me fuzzy socks and cookie dough?" I giggle, wiggling my toes. A warmth spirals inside, dulling my pain and sensibilities all at once.

A nervous energy flickers over Seth's face. He rubs the back of his head, coloring rushing to his cheeks. "You know, I think I have the skills to do that in the real world, too. Would you still want to stick around with me then?"

I want to reassure and assuage his anxiety that I'll want him in the real world. Because I will. I know I've wanted him there, loved him there for so long, even when I fiercely denied it. But I'm worried that admiration won't run both ways. What if he fell in love with a version of me in this world, but that's not who Madeline Finch is? What happens when I become all the things he hates again?

I have no intention of going back to who I was completely, but some things aren't as easy to erase when they're grounded in the storyline, parts of me that people will expect and try to hold me to, and it'll be a slower change.

"I want that, you know. But maybe we shouldn't make any promises to each other until we're back and settled. This whole thing has been very disorienting," I say with a yawn.

Seth drops his head, and I fight the pull to comfort him. I'm too drowsy, and I need to sleep more than anything. "Why don't you shut your eyes for a bit? There should be fresh-baked cookies when you wake up, okay?"

"That sounds fantastic," I mumble. "Thank you."

Huh. Maybe I could be good at this whole being alone together thing.

## CHAPTER SEVENTEEN
# The Holiday
### SETH

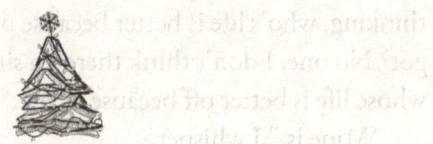

THE MOVIE *It's a Wonderful Life* is one of my family's "no matter what" holiday traditions.

Even if my mom had to work the late shifts at the steakhouse she worked in, known for its holiday decorations and overcrowded in December.

Even the year my dad left us with a note that just had one word on it, "Sorry," and never came back.

Even the year of my accident, my mother made sure they put it on my TV in the hospital, and she sat, crocheting a pair of useless, fingerless mittens next to me while it was on.

With romance, humor, and a reminder that even when everything looks bleak, there's a life worth living, the movie has a little of everything.

So when I heard Maddie had never seen it, it didn't take long before I found it on a streaming service we had and booted that bad boy up so we could watch it with some warm chocolate chip cookies and hot cocoa.

As the movie fades out to the tune of *Auld Lang Syne*, I peek down at her, resting her head on a pillow on my lap, and brush a piece of hair out of her face with my thumb. "Hey? What's going on in that head of yours? I can feel the cogs whirring from here." I trace the curve of her jaw, trailing the pad of my thumb down her neck, trying to calm the melancholy radiating off of her.

"It's nothing. I just—um." She worries the bottom of her lip with her teeth.

"It's not supposed to be sad at the end," I murmur.

"I know. I just—it just got me thinking about how this would translate into my life. You know, the whole ripple effect thing. His existence was so important to so many people. And it got me thinking, who's life is better because of me? And you know what I got? No one. I don't think there's a single person in the real world whose life is better off because of me."

"Mine is," I whisper.

"Only recently."

"It's still a part of our life, though." I shrug. "I'm not going to sugarcoat anything and pretend like there aren't some things that I disagree with in your past, just like I have skeletons and versions of me I'm not proud of. But Maddie, there's still a lot of life left for us to live, and you can make it whatever you want, regardless of who you've been. Identity isn't a permanent thing, you know? We can change."

"I'm going to try my best to make things right."

"I know you will." I rest my hand on her side. In the past month, I've seen a lot of different versions of Madeline Finch, but this is the one that terrifies me more than anything because I'm pretty sure this is the real one, and I'm fucking head over heels in love with her.

I'm working on trusting her, but I still haven't been honest about my past. Not that she's asked, but when she's commented on my tattoos, tracing and swirling a finger around them, I haven't worked up the courage to tell her those exist in the real world too. Or when she makes a joke about me being athletic, and I want to shout, *I'm actually ridiculously athletic in the real world too, and I was one of the top quarterbacks in the nation, sweetheart. I just didn't have the drive to rehab my knee after the people around me shattered my heart.*

I want to share everything with her, but something's holding me back. I don't know if it's fear or hesitation over the past versions of who she's been.

Maddie's hand tightens around my waist and nuzzles her head into my side. "Thank you for coming over. I really do appreciate it."

"Of course, Buttercup." I rake my fingers slowly through her hair, relishing the silky feel of it against my skin.

"But why the hell did you bring Jenny to the skating rink?" she mumbles.

I swallow. The answer to that question is probably why I haven't shared the details of my past with her. "Because I do foolish things when I'm scared, Maddie."

"What were you scared of?"

There's a beat where I have a choice. I could run again. I could lie. I could redirect the subject. She's out of it enough that she probably wouldn't even call me out, but there's something inside of me screaming, don't you dare run from her this time.

"I'm scared of how much I've fallen in love with you."

A tiny "oh" passes over Maddie's lips. She lifts her head, and when I meet her stare, she's searching my face for what I don't know—I'd give her the answer to whatever it is if I did.

"What's up?" I ask.

"Nothing, it's just, can you remind me you said that tomorrow? My memory is terrible on these meds."

I brush a piece of hair out of her face and lean forward to press a kiss to her temple. "I'll remind you every day if you let me."

"Yes, Seth Aarons. You can confess your undying love for me daily if you must." She giggles, readjusting her head on my lap. "I love you too, you know." She hums with a yawn, turning back on her side.

"Maddie? Can I ask you something too?"

"Of course, you can."

"What happened to you and Jenny? Why did you?" I stutter, trying to find the right words.

"Become a heinous bitch?"

"I probably would have gone with softer words there." I snort.

"It's not a good reason." She shifts on the couch. The blanket on her shoulder drops, and I pull it back up. "Now that I've had time where I'm not constantly drowning in my bad decision, I know that."

"It's still a reason."

"Right, well, if you really want to know."

"I do. I want to know all of you if you'll let me."

*Hypocrite, why don't you share your past?*

"So, for the end of my First-Year, beginning of my sophomore, I dated this guy named Brady. I was head-over-heels, picking out a wedding dress, in love—even if now I couldn't tell you why. He was my first. Penetrative sex hurt, but it always does when you're just starting out, right? So we kept pushing through, but it never got better, and I required a lot of foreplay to get anywhere—you maybe have noticed that last part already."

"Noticed, adored, whatever you want to call it."

"Right." She snorts.

"I'm serious, Buttercup. Any man that wouldn't love making you make those sounds is a complete fool."

Her cheeks flush, but she keeps her stare trained on the plate of cookies on the coffee table like she needs a spot to focus that isn't me while she's being this vulnerable. "Well, Brady didn't see things that way but thank you. So one day right before Thanksgiving break, while we were in bed, he got frustrated with all the work, and while I was legs up, underpants down, he looked at me and said, 'Look, you're cute and all, Maddie, but you're not worth the hassle.' And then he left.

"That's how the asshole broke up with me.

"I was devastated and probably could and should have just stayed broken, but a week later, Jenny took me out for milkshakes.

She said she wanted me to meet someone, but whoever it was never showed up—that information's not important, so ignore the drug-induced tangent, but anyway—Brady walked in with his new girlfriend, Lacey Cane, and hell, she was gorgeous. Brady knew it, too. He treated her so differently from me. And I just knew if I ever wanted someone to follow me around and look at me like Brady did with Lacey, then I'd have to become someone like her, you know?"

"You know what he was doing wasn't love, right?" I swallow down a ball of guilt threatening to lodge itself permanently in my throat. Maddie wasn't the only one scared of never being loved again that week. Her timeline matches those first few moments I saw her. The one where I was studying with Jenny, and she was broken in the kitchen, and then, of course, the diner, when I chickened out and never went to the table to meet them.

I was the person who never came that day.

What would have happened if I had found the courage to approach her?

Would we have become friends?

Would she still have gone down the Mean Girl road?

Timing is a fickle thing.

One extra second, and I don't get hit by a truck.

I don't go to Ephron University.

I don't meet Jenny.

I don't meet Maddie.

Ten minutes at a diner where I swallow my pride and bumble around the girl of my dreams, and maybe this would have been how we spent every Friday night.

"Anyway." She snuggles further into me. "It's not like he was wrong. I was pretty cute then, but cute and soft only get you so far."

"You were perfect. You know what I said when I first saw you?"

"At the party? I've got nothing if it's not the word 'no.'"

Shit, so I said that out loud then.

"Not at the party. That's the first time we met, but the first time I saw you was at your apartment. I was studying with Jenny, and you were making tea in the kitchen, oblivious to my existence. But fuck Maddie, I sure the hell was aware of you. Every single one of your movements, I watched you so fucking gone already, and the words 'holy shirtballs, that is the most beautiful woman I have ever seen' fell out of my lips."

"Is that really what you thought?"

"Would I lie about saying the word 'shirtballs'?"

Her lip quivers. "But you hated me. You wouldn't even shake my hand when you saw me. You said 'no.'"

"I wasn't saying 'no' to you, Buttercup. I was saying 'no' to what I wanted to do to you."

I hear her throat work. "What did you want to do to me?"

"I didn't even know you, but I wanted to tug you close and kiss you so hard you'd forget your name, and that terrified me."

"Can I tell you a secret?"

"Please."

"The first time I met you. I wouldn't have minded."

# CHAPTER EIGHTEEN
# Santa Claus is Comin' to Town
### MADDIE

"YOU OKAY, BUTTERCUP?" Green eyes sparkle with power hovering over me as the world's most kissable bee-stung lips curve into a smug, satisfied smirk.

Ass.

Hell, I love this man.

Seth hasn't left my side since the flare started. Making me breakfast in the morning, lunch, and dinner, making me copious amounts of tea, and holding my hair when the pain is too much, and I find myself with my head in the toilet. Even Connor's warming up to him after how wonderful he's been for the last three days.

And I have to admit; for someone so keen on never having anyone see this side of me, it's pretty fucking fantastic to have someone rub my back when I'm sobbing through a mercy-kill stab or wrap me up in his arms when I get a cold flash.

Today, I'm finally feeling better, so I started this whole make-out session as a thank you, but it quickly turned into Seth dominating the situation like he always does.

Which is the worst.

In the best kind of way.

"I'm fine." I breathe out, careful not to give in to the primal urge coiling deep inside, begging me to let go and frantically kiss the crap out of him.

His ego's big enough as is.

"Until Christmas, this pussy is mine. Understood?" he says, slowly peeling off my underwear. His fingers graze along the top of my thigh, leaving a crackling fire in their wake along my skin.

I nod, burying my lips behind the whites of my teeth. "Yes, sir."

"Good girl." His palm slides along my curves toward my breast. With every inch, I surrender more to him, desperate for his touch to set me ablaze. It's dangerous, sure, but playing with fire is getting to be an addiction I don't want to break.

He strokes my nipple with the pad of his finger, and my back arches at the sensation. A breathy cry crashes over my lips.

"That sound is mine." His tongue lashes against the sensitive peak of my breast. "You, Madeline Finch, are mine. Is that clear?"

"I'd agree for a price," I say between heaving breaths.

"Name it, anything," he says in a hushed whisper. With gentle reverence, he takes my breast and strokes my sensitive peak in a slow, deliberate manner. "God, you're beautiful, you know that?"

"I thought I was cute." I snort.

"Darling, you're everything."

His fingers explore my curves as he whispers exaltations into my skin as if this bedroom is a place of worship and my body is the altar. As if he's found a non-verbal way to tell me I might be worth something like this, after all.

Like none of this is a hassle to him, but rather the most important thing he's ever done.

That this time spent with me is worth everything.

"Seth, I want you to make me beg again."

He pauses his worshipping, picking his head up and studying me. "I couldn't have heard you right. I'm sorry. What do you want?"

"Seth Aarons, demolish me."

Okay. I know, I know. I'm all for advancing women's rights, and I promise I'm not turning the clock back fifty years with this request. But here's the thing, after the past few weeks, I can safely say I've never been in love, and I'm obsessed with the feeling.

Toe-curling. Butterflies. An incomparable warmth.

It's intoxicating, and unfortunately, when Seth has me begging, I have the strongest orgasms of my life. So who's to judge what gets me off in the bedroom? I'll be the tough, badass woman on the streets and thoroughly wrecked in the sheets. Is that so bad?

"I can do that, baby." He smiles. "If you're sure, I won't take it easy on you just because you asked nicely." He reaches for the oil resting on the top of my nightstand. I wasn't subtle when I started kissing him about where I intended this whole thing to go.

"I'd respect you less if you did."

Warmth gathers between my thighs in anticipation as Seth squeezes some CBD oil onto his fingers. Light streams through the cracks of the blinds, catching his shirtless torso at all angles.

I don't know if there's an unflattering angle for this man, but this isn't one of them. I reach out, tracing the swirls of his tattoo. I've grown inexplicably attached to the black ink on his chest, and right arm like it's a part of him, so I naturally have to love it, but it'll be gone in a week.

His lips twitch with a satisfied smile at the brush of my fingers. "Fuck, you feel good," he whispers.

"I wish you could feel what it's like when you touch me down there."

"Trust me. I have some idea." He winks. With an incredible gentleness, Seth slides his oiled finger into my entrance, swirling around and dragging my wetness up and over my clit. "Always so ready for me."

He continues with his slow, gentle strokes, and I close my eyes, savoring his fingers. "Thank you for taking your time with me," I whisper.

"Baby, you don't have to thank me for anything." He brushes

my hair out of my face and traces my jaw with his thumb. A tender gaze blazes over my skin. "But if you want to thank me after I'm done blowing your mind, that's fine."

"So cocky." I click my tongue.

"Sure am." He smirks, watching my breaths and matching the speed of his finger to my needs. I writhe under him, trying to bring his mouth to mine. He presses a kiss to the corner of my lips, and it's not enough. A whimper escapes, and he chuckles, brushing his nose down the nape of my neck. Nipping and licking along the way.

He keeps to his quiet exploration of my body as my breaths slow and the pressure between my thighs becomes unbearable.

"Seth." His name escapes in an exalting breath.

"Fuck, I love the way you say my name." He pauses on my stomach, biting the skin below my belly button, and I let out a little yelp.

In the past three weeks, we've done this dance far more times than my dignity would care to admit, but never with him this open with his feelings for me. It's an odd comfort to have him on this side with me like suddenly the flames licking and singing all of my nerve ends aren't as dangerous like they're no longer an uncontained wildfire, but the life-giving warmth of a fire crackling in the hearth in an icy world.

With a slow drag of his finger, he pulls out the one teasing my apex and pins a heated stare on me. Uh oh.

"Suck on my fingers, Madeline." He puts them near my mouth.

"What? No way." I laugh.

"I'm just doing what you asked for," he says in a low murmur.

I sit up a bit, meeting his fingers and wrapping my mouth around them. Sweetness and a little salt hit my tastebuds. "Do you see how good you taste?" he asks as he pulls my fingers out in a slow, agonizing manner.

I whimper as the pads of his middle and forefinger drag across my lower lip, and the urge to be satisfied becomes almost unbearable.

"I'm famished for it." His eyes twinkle with that power I've grown accustomed to, and suddenly I don't fear it. He drags my legs to the edge of the bed, burying his head between my thighs.

I let out a shuddering gasp when his tongue finds my clit and lashes against it. Lines of mirth edge his eyes and deepen with each reaction his tongue against my bud elicits. Clutching his silky curls, I mutter my praises for him.

"Seth—I—" I stutter, fighting against my last wall of defense. I want to let go and be totally vulnerable, let myself be a writhing, whimpering mess, undone by his mouth. But there's still the part of me that doesn't find doing something like that particularly easy.

"It's okay, you're safe with me," he whispers like he knows what's on my mind. "I promise, whatever shit we're doing, however much we play, you will always be safe with me. Now, surrender to me, Madeline, please. Please give me that. I need it."

Seth's words are exactly what I need to drop that last wall because I'll do just about anything to make him happy.

His warm mouth wraps around my clit, and that's enough to break me.

With a whimper, I writhe underneath him, fisting the sheets. "Fuck, Seth. I love you so fucking much. Please. Pressure. Please." I beg.

He slips a finger into my entrance, flickering on my g-spot, but it's not enough. "More, please."

"Patience, Buttercup. I can't stretch you out all at once. You know that."

"I don't care what I can't do. I need you."

I'm out of my head, devoid of thought, and every part of me is burning with the need to be pile driven by that man. My libido is at war with any form of common sense I own, but I don't care.

There will be times when the pain outweighs my needs that I choose it instead, but there are times too, when what I want and need seem greater, and that's my choice. I get to control this aspect, even when I can't control other parts.

And right now, when I'm so fucking alive and threatening to collapse into an uncontrollable horny mess, that's the decision I want to make.

"I don't want your fingers. I need you," I whimper. "Please."

He flicks his tongue, too slow, too little pressure and I tighten and writhe under him, breathing heavily with Seth's name and tongue the only thing on my mind.

"I don't want to hurt you." He shakes his head, pressing his hand into my hip bone, and I can't handle not being filled with him anymore. It's literal torture.

"Seth." I reach out, trying to present a coherent argument for Team Fuck-Me. "This damn thing has taken so much from me, and sometimes I want to take something back. I want to be with you right now. You and I know there's a ring inside that drawer you sometimes use to help, please."

"Are you sure?"

"Positive."

Slowly, he pulls his fingers out, lashing against my clit one last time, and then goes into the drawer and fishes out a green rubber ring. He glances at me and blushes.

"You okay there, Aarons?" I cock my head to the side, feeling very naked, and draw the blanket to my chest.

He stares at me with an endearing smirk. "Just imprinting this moment into my memory. Fuck, you're beautiful." He leans in and presses a slow, savoring, worshipping kiss on my lips before pulling away and rubbing the back of his head. "I uh."

Anxiety roils in the pit of my stomach, but it doesn't feel like it belongs to me.

"Are you nervous?"

"You're still very intimidating if you hadn't noticed." His cheeks burn a brighter red.

"My poor baby, come here." I smile, crooking my finger in that come hither manner.

He climbs over me, handing me a condom and the rubber ring, and I slide both over the length of his erection.

He takes a water-based lube and ensures I'm good and ready before slowly pushing in. "Okay?" he asks, watching my expression with a wary one of his own.

I bite my bottom lip and hum an "mhm," sighing as the pressure fills me.

"I *am* yours, you know." He brushes my hair out of my face and lays a soft kiss on my lips with a thrust of his hips.

It takes a second for me to adjust to the fill of him, to the pressure, but when I hear those words, I know I can't hold back anymore. "Don't be gentle," I whisper. "I'm begging you."

And that's all it takes for him to lose it on me and melt away any sign of the controlled, pretentious man I've sparred with for the last two years. With each pump inside of me, Seth grows increasingly unguarded. He captures my mouth with his like he's a man starved.

His finger finds my clit again, and I tighten until I'm screaming and fairly sure I'm about to have the strongest orgasm of my entire life.

He writhes on top of me, shuddering with a "fuck," his pumps becoming sloppier and sloppier until neither of us can handle it anymore. I claw into his back and let out an earth-shattering scream I'm sure frightened the winter birds in the tree outside, and Seth releases, collapsing against my chest with a chuckle.

"What." I push his shoulder as he buries his lips into my neck and catches his breath. "It's not nice to laugh at someone after you have sex with them."

"I'm sorry, it's just. Fuck, you're a loud one." He teases.

"Yeah, but you're mine." I beam, equally breathless. "Now let me go pee, and maybe you can be a good little sub for once." I pat his cheek.

"Yes, Ms. Finch, I suppose I could do that." He flutters his inky eyelashes at me, and I snort.

Getting out of bed, I squeeze my thighs together and walk to the bathroom attached to my room. Passing my dresser, I catch a glimpse of the hourglass Ellie gave me, the snow inside swirling like a blizzard. A pang of guilt tightens in my chest. I'm not going to use the ten minutes anymore, but I still owe Seth that story. Soon.

I don't want to mess up our little slice of heaven.

## CHAPTER NINETEEN
# Love, Actually
### SETH

"YOU DON'T LIKE IT." Maddie frowns, her eyes moving down a clean version of my jersey, falling so it hits just below her ass.

My stomach twists itself into knots.

I was never one to be encumbered with pre-game nerves, a fact that translated to this world when I played one of the biggest bowl games of the year with a clear head and steady hands. But now, in my hotel room, I can't stop my hands from tremoring. I try to draw moisture to my throat as Maddie's figure grows more self-conscious by the minute. "No, it's not that."

"I just thought where this is our last day, and you seemed to enjoy the whole being quarterback thing, that this might be special. I mean, Connor—not that I mean to bring him up—but he liked it when I did this. But I can feel you, and I know I messed up somehow. I'm sorry. I'll—I'll take it off." She twists her fingers in the hem of the jersey.

I want to stop her, tell her that it's a lovely jersey and that in any other instance, I would fling her over my shoulder and slam her on the bed, but I can't, not today. Because Maddie's right, if what Ellie said to me, and it seems her as well, is correct, we're going back to the real world tomorrow. A world where the only thing to my name is massive student loan debt. I'm not the star quarterback I used to be or have been here, and I'm anxious that Maddie doesn't understand that. And I'm still trying not to read too into the fact that she didn't give me an answer when I mentioned us doing whatever this is in the real world. I've been left because I didn't carry that status anymore, and what I had with Kennedy has nothing on the bond that's developed between Maddie and me.

I don't know that I'll be able to handle it if I'm not enough for her anymore.

It's a fear that's been rooted deep down for days, and I need to talk it out before the weed grows.

Maddie drags the jersey over her head, getting stuck in the shirt's hole, and I rescue her. "Who taught you how to take off a shirt?"

"I'm not good at pulling things out of holes. Sue me," she huffs. She meets my stare when she's freed, and her lips twitch at her joke. But I don't have it in me to return the smile, the anxiety roiling deep inside growing too strong for much of anything. I'm a statue of fear. "Seth, what's going on?" she whispers. "You won. I thought you'd be happy. I thought you'd want to celebrate."

"This isn't me," I manage.

"What do you mean?"

"What happens tomorrow? When I'm just Lumberjack Frasier?"

"Oh, is that what you're worried about?" With an incredible gentleness, Maddie cradles my face with her hands. "I promise, I don't care about this whole football thing Seth. I love *you*. You're the one who takes great care of me when I don't feel well and is secretly way funnier than I want to ever admit out loud. And I know that you're also smart, kind, loyal, and fiercely protective. Is any of that going to change tomorrow?"

"Well, no." I breathe out, my lungs expanding a fraction with her reassurances.

"Then you should cross that worry right off. I'm not going

anywhere as long as you want me." Her finger comes up, and she traces the swirl of the ink on my chest. "I will miss these just a little, though."

Tattoos that exist on my body in the real world, too. Tattoos she won't understand if I don't tell her the damn truth. I don't want to start tomorrow with her finding out that I hid a significant part of my past from her. It's now or never.

"I need to tell you something."

"Oh, yeah, what's up?" She bounces on her toes, and yeah, taking the jersey off to have this conversation was a bad idea because Maddie's perfect breasts are so close, and I'd much rather have my mouth wrapped as far as it'll go around them instead of having this deep conversation.

"Maybe we get a shirt on you first." I blush.

"Right. Right." She giggles, walking over to her daisy duffel bag and pulling something out. She tosses it over her head and sits on the bed with her legs crossed, wearing the Nar Wars shirt she wore the night I went to her house. "I thought I'd wear it tonight where you liked it so much." She shrugs with a timid smirk.

"It's my favorite." I smile, but it doesn't reach my eyes. "Maddie, I haven't been entirely honest with you." I rub the back of my neck, pacing the length of the room, counting the squares on the carpet print with each long, quick stride. "It's just... there are things...about my past..."

"What about it?"

"Uhm. Do you remember when Connor swore he played football against me at the store, and then I started acting weird?"

"Yeah, you dropped a ton of books and were weirder than normal. What gives?"

"Connor was right. We did play each other a few years ago. And it's not a part of my past that I like reliving, or it wasn't until all of this." I gesture to the room around us.

"Wait. Are you telling me Lumberjack Fraser played football *—collegiately*?"

"Um, yeah. And I was good too." I smile, remembering the

constant high from my four-plus touchdown games, letting the ball soar through the air and nail one of my teammates forty yards down the field. It was a feeling I soaked in today, never taking a single moment of that time on the field for granted because, for once, I knew it would be my last. "Ellie didn't embellish much of anything. This is how my life should have been."

"What happened?"

I rub the back of my head and exhale. "I got hit by a truck."

"I'm sorry. You, what?" Maddie shrieks, jumping up from the bed. "Oh my god, are you okay?" She grabs hold of my arms, twisting and turning them like she's inspecting for bruises like I'm telling her the accident just happened.

"I'm mean, you've seen me, Mads. I'm fine now." I cradle her cheek in my hand, trying to quiet her own sudden spiking anxiety. "I promise. It's just that I lost everything when it happened. My future career. My scholarship. My girlfriend I was going to propose to—you ever heard of Kennedy Spruce?"

"The influencer?"

I nod with a blush. "That was my girlfriend."

Maddie blinks. "I'm sorry, I couldn't have heard you right. Are you saying you, Seth Aarons, the man who nicknamed me Satanic Barbie, dated *the* Kennedy Spruce?"

"Mhm, for five years, and when it was pretty clear I couldn't play anymore, she dumped my ass."

"And I was a Kennedy clone." Maddie gently grasps my hand and rubs a circle into my palm with her thumb. "No wonder you were hesitant to get to know me." She massages the tendon on the inside of my wrist, tracing the black ink there. "Wait, so are these real?"

"You like these, huh?" I chuckle, taking both her hands with mine.

"Mmm." She hums. "Maybe a little, but I'd be okay if you had a blank canvas too."

I dip down and press a kiss to her lips. "They're mine. They're real. I got them after I signed my letter of intent and wanted to celebrate."

A little giggle bubbles over her. A wrinkle scrunches her nose. And I want to scoop her up and slam her down on the bed.

"What's so funny?" I kiss her neck, asking with each passing giggle.

"Nothing. I'm just thinking about how funny it would have been to meet that Seth Aarons. Lord, that Maddie would have been so intimidated."

"Yeah?" I smile, walking her back toward the bed, a weight lifting off my chest. "And what about now?"

"Very relaxed around you now." She nips at my bottom lip. "You're a teddy bear, really."

"Mmm," I hum against my lips, "I'll have to see if I can change that then."

I push her onto the bed, and she puts a hand out to stop me. "I need to tell you something too. I—um, I did something bad." She avoids my eye, chewing on her lip, and again, I feel the anxiety spike between us.

"Whatever it is, Maddie, it'll be okay."

"It's just. I made a deal with Ellie when we first got here." She pulls at her fingertips.

My stomach sinks. "What kind of deal?"

"So before you freak out, I swear I'm not using it, but she made this deal that if I got you to fall in love with me, I could have ten minutes of my life to do over."

My jaw tightens as she continues.

"And I know it wasn't right, but I don't care about it anymore. I need you to know that, okay?"

"What were you going to use the ten minutes for, Madeline?" I rub my hand along my jaw, and an unwelcome anger boils in the pit of my stomach. I've protected myself from falling in love with Madeline for a reason, and now that I've let my guard down, she's standing in front of me, telling me she orchestrated it for some deal?

"I um. I thought I could stop you from entering my bedroom so Connor wouldn't break up with me."

"Fuck, of course you did." I rake a hand through my curls and pace along the room.

"But I swear, Seth. I don't want to use it anymore—and I didn't—"

"So this past week, what was that? Just bullshit?"

"No, of course not, Seth—please—" She gets up to take my hands, and I step away.

Part of me wants to tell her it's okay. I understand we were different people at the beginning of all of this. But after the jersey, my anxiety is too high to deal with this properly.

"I need a second," I grit out, and without another word, I march through the bedroom door and shut it behind me.

---

**TEN MINUTES** in the frigid night air is all I need to realize that I'm not upset with Maddie. Heck, who am I kidding? I would have done the same thing if it had been offered to me.

Ten minutes can change a lot, even though it feels like an insignificant amount of time. The ripple effect can be massive.

On my way back to the hotel, I stopped in a little café to pick up a hot chocolate as a peace offering, willing the elevator to move just a little faster.

"Buttercup, I'm sorry." I swing open the hotel door, but I don't sense her in the room. "Buttercup?" I ask in vain. She's not here. I know that, but hope is a fickle thing too.

A note sits on the nightstand beside the bed with some weird hourglass snow globe. Glitter swirls inside like a miniature blizzard.

*Seth,*

*Take the ten minutes, go back and wait a minute to cross the street.*

*Get the life back you deserve.*

*Look me up sometime when you have a game nearby.*

*I'm sorry. I love you.*

My lips curve into a smile. If I'm being honest, getting hit by the truck isn't the regret I have, as awesome as the past four weeks have been, because it brought me Jenny and Maddie, and it brought me perspective.

But I have one regret about a gorgeous woman at a diner.

And that one I very much intend to fix.

Ten minutes, right? That's all it takes.

## CHAPTER TWENTY
# Last Christmas
### MADDIE

IF I HADN'T JUST SPENT the last month in a town ripped right out of a freaking Hallmark movie, I probably would have freaked the fuck out when I woke up this morning in the middle of a diner that shuttered its doors two years ago.

"Earth to Pookie. You okay?"

Jenny's hand waves in my face and brings my attention to focus. Her brow furrows under her baseball cap, staring at me.

Aw, hell, I've missed her.

"Sorry." I blink a few times, trying to figure out where in my timeline I am. "I, um, I'm just tired today."

"Still not sleeping, huh?" She reaches out and grabs my hand. "I love you, boo. But he's not worth losing sleep over. I promise you'll get over this, find someone who deserves you."

Oh hell. I know what this is. This is the day Brady and Lacey taught me a lesson.

Logically, I feel like this timeline doesn't make sense, that wherever Seth is, he should have already been hit by the truck, but whatever he did with his ten minutes, I'll endure this moment with grace as long as he is happy. And maybe, I can make something right of my life too.

Jenny brings her lips to her straw, blowing bubbles into the milkshake and giggling. I cradle my head in my hands and admire the warmth and joy hanging in Jenny's eyes.

Gosh, she's as radiant as the freaking sun.

"What are you looking at, weirdo?" She laughs.

"You. You're pretty."

Sweet Jenny, who doesn't know the betrayal I'm capable of, doesn't know how easily I tossed a fifteen-year friendship for nothing. A Jenny who didn't do the same to me.

I reach out and grab her face. "I love you, Pixie. And I'm so so grateful for you. I'd never do anything to lose that, understood? You are cherished and magical, and I love your face."

"I'm grateful for you too. Why are you squishing my cheeks?" She mumbles, her eyes glancing at her phone.

I release her cheeks and take a sip of my milkshake, savoring the freezing chocolate cream sliding down my throat—the frostiest thing here.

"Oh, here he is!" Jenny waves at someone, wiggling in the booth.

My heart stops. We didn't meet anyone that day. It was just us. "Seth, over here!"

I can't bring my gaze to meet his. My heart hammers in my chest like it's trying to escape, like it knows its other half is here and can't wait to be whole again.

Instead, I keep my stare angled at the floor and catch a knee brace over a pair of grey sweatpants.

"Maddie, this is my friend Seth."

With incredible strength, I pick my stare up from the ground and meet Seth Aarons in all his sharp angles and dimpled chin glory. His emerald eyes land on mine with a crooked grin. "Hello," he says with a tip of his chin.

I go to open my mouth. Hello is an easy word. I should be able to utter it, but I can't—. There's a decided twinkle in his eye when he sees the effect his presence here has on me, and the words 'ass' want to fall out of my lips, but I don't know if Jenny would quite get my sudden annoyance with our guest.

"Maddie. Scoot." Jenny gestures for me to move. "I have the purses. Seth has to sit next to you."

"Oh, right." I blink, trying to shake myself out of my haze, and push along the bench.

Seth slides in, and I sit rigidly in the booth. Heat radiates off the side of him.

"Maddie, this is my friend Seth I was telling you about. We're in Chemistry class together. He just transferred here, so I thought we should invite him into the pack since we're the two coolest people on campus."

"Oh yeah?" I nervously laugh, turning my head toward him. "It's nice to meet you, Seth."

"Likewise, Maddie, was it?"

"Mhm." I manage. When I left Seth, he was angry, justifiably so—but if this is the ten minutes he's choosing to redo, then we're probably okay, right?

Jenny's lips curl, but they soon falter, following someone who just entered the diner.

I don't have to guess—I know it's Brady and Lacey. He'll walk past our booth ignoring us soon, pretending we didn't date for almost a year, and I'll get the idea that I need to be more like Lacey. Except my head is so scattered with thoughts of Seth that I doubt that the second part will happen now. Not that I want it to. I meant it when I told Seth that the regretful version of me was never anyone's saving grace.

I leave my hand resting on the bench for stability. When this happened the first time, my heart was ripped out of my chest, but I'm not even sure my heart is mine to lose anymore.

Right on schedule, a calm, cool, collected woman saunters past our booth, Brady following two steps behind. "Babe, I want curly fries."

"I'll order whatever you want when the waitress comes, babe."

"No, I want them now. I'm starving."

"Of course, anything you want." He scratches the back of his head and turns to go to the counter, not bothering to meet my eye.

Flames lick the nerves along my hand. I glance down and find Seth's pinky brushing up against mine. His sleeves are rolled up to his elbows, and the ink on his right arm swirls around his forearms. He flashes me a tentative smile.

"I need to go pee," Jenny exclaims, pulling us away from our weird stare. "Maddie, tell Seth about the matching shirts we just got or something." She glances between us and mouths *he's cute. Go for it.*

God, I love that woman.

She bolts out of the booth and disappears, leaving the two of us behind.

"Matching shirts? Huh?" He arches his brow, still stroking my pinky. Butterflies swarm the pit of my stomach.

"Club tees with narwhals." I nod. "We can get you one, if you want, to be a part of the club. Where we're going to be pals, friends, companions."

With a heated stare, Seth locks his eyes with mine. "I'm not here to be just friends with you, Madeline."

"Oh then, why are you here?" My pulse thuds in my ears, and I squirm on the bench, the rush of sensations overwhelming me.

Seth cocks his head to the side. "Am I making you nervous?" His lips curl into a tiny smirk.

"What?" I laugh, and in my panic, a snort follows. I cover my mouth. "Hell, so much for getting rid of that tic."

"Oh, come on, it's cute."

"Well, fair, that's what I am now." I huff.

Two fingers tuck under my chin and lift them. "You're everything. I knew you'd be here and still barely found the courage to walk over."

Seth's gaze lands on my lips, and he raises a brow for permission. "Please," I whisper. His mouth molds over mine, and my whole body sighs with that coming home to a warm fire feeling.

His hand tangles in my mess of hair, and I thread my fingers through the curls in the back of his head.

"This is going to change a lot," I whisper against his lips. "What if we don't make it? What if—"

"Don't worry, Buttercup." He presses our foreheads together. "Whatever it is when we wake up, I'll find you. Okay? We could live a thousand lives, and I'd find you in all of them."

"Whoa, your bond worked fast," Jenny squeaks with a huge grin plastered on her face a few feet away. "I knew it was a special one."

And Seth and I deteriorate into a giggling, happily ever after mess.

## CHAPTER TWENTY-ONE
# The Family Man
### SETH

"SHIT, THIS WAS A BAD FUCKING IDEA," I grumble, scraping burnt bits of egg in the pan into the trash.

"Dude, relax. It's not like we haven't made a shitty breakfast for them before." Connor rubs my shoulders, and I breathe a little lighter. Connor may have made Jenny breakfast before in the house we share with them, but I haven't done this for Maddie, not like this.

This morning, I debated just laying in bed with her and never leaving. Sure Ellie made a mistake, but when the fresh memories flooded in, I saw how much ten minutes can change a life's course. Maddie and I became inseparable after the diner. I didn't think it was possible to love her more than I already did, but since we met in this timeline, the bond between us has increased every day, and I've grown more and more irrevocably hers.

Jenny and Maddie stayed rooming together, and eventually, I moved in. Jenny still tutored Connor, but without a barrier like Maddie, they got cozy pretty damn fast. And apparently, Connor being here motivated me to play football again. Not in a collegiate way. The knee's still toast, but I can do the club flag team fine, and I go over the tape and game-day strategies with Coach and

Connor once a week for "fun." In another semester, we can call it what it is. I'm the quarterback coach.

"What are you doing?" I nod to his phone, pushing the sleeves of my crewneck up, not hiding my tattoos or moderately toned forearms for once.

"Ordering delivery that the girls always let us pass off as food we made, even though they know it's from Slow Drip like I always do after you burn the eggs." He shrugs.

"I always liked you."

"Thank you?" He chuckles. "Why are you being so weird today?"

"Just nervous."

"Oh shit, no way. Are you proposing today?"

"Not a great day to do it." I shake my head. "Probably should save that for a while down the road."

Soft footsteps pad down the hallway, and I breathe a sigh of relief when Jenny appears around the corner. I need to collect myself before Maddie sees me like this, or I'll never hear the end of how nervous I was the first day.

"Why wouldn't it be good?" Jenny smirks, curling into Connor's lap on a stool. "I thought we had decided Christmas Eve was the perfect day to do it."

"The day for what?" A honey-sweet voice makes me jump, and I end up knocking my mound of burnt toast.

Jenny studies the burnt toast with disgust. "You two usually have the delivery here by now. What gives?"

"Aarons seems extra nervous today or something."

"Does he?" Maddie quirks her head, and I get the complete picture of her in my flannel and a pair of boxer shorts poking through. "Regrets, Aarons?"

"Not a fucking one," I say, suddenly famished in a way that breakfast can't satisfy. In a second, I hoist her over my shoulder and take the stairs two at a time.

"We'll leave your breakfast in the fridge for y'all, Pookie," Jenny hollers.

"Thank you, Pixie," the woman thrust over my shoulder returns with a giggle.

## CHAPTER TWENTY-TWO
# It's a Wonderful Life
### MADDIE

SETH SOMEHOW LIES me both gently and hungrily on the bed. "Boxers." He orders, tugging his shirt off in one swift motion.

"What if this Maddie doesn't enjoy being bossed around?" I smirk.

"Sweetheart." He pins a stare on me. "We have the same memories in here, right?"

I blush. Vivid pictures of Seth driving me to the brink every damn time take center stage.

"Thought so." He smirks, climbing over me.

"Written by a woman." I shake my head.

"Studied the classics." He returns. "I worked hard to be this good. I'll have you know."

"You know how many buttons were on this flannel—I had to button them all."

"You really didn't...." With an hungered frenzy, he rips the shirt off me, buttons flying everywhere. "You could have stayed up here. I would have brought you breakfast in bed, provided dessert." He presses a kiss to my collarbone.

"I didn't know if you had gotten freaked out and run away." I drag my teeth over my bottom lip.

"I told you I'd find you, Maddie, and I meant it. I'm yours. However you want me. To do whatever. Shatter me. If I only have today with you like this, I don't fucking care."

His lips capture mine, soothing all my worries away. With each pass of his lips, he reassures me with quiet whispers that tell their truths in the heat of his kiss.

*I am cherished.*

*I am loved.*

And for the first time in forever, I know without a doubt that I am enough, as I am now.

God bless Ellie, everyone.

# Acknowledgments

After writing an overly verbose acknowledgment section for my book "Finding Gene Kelly," you'd think I'd run out of people to thank.

But I could write a novella—nay, a Maas-size series, about all the people I'm thankful for. Would it have significantly fewer faeries? Sure. But it'd be no less magical since the people who fill my life are undoubtedly the most magical group of individuals I could have been blessed with.

So if you are here reading this. I want to thank you, with everything I have and a chocolate chip cookie on top, for being on this journey with me. Thank you for yelling enthusiastically about my books.

Thank you for the posts. For the DMs. For the e-mails. Thank you for telling your friends. I appreciate you so so so incredibly much.

Thank you to everyone who read an early copy of this story (even the ones that ran off to Europe) Morgan, Jo, Laurie, Zoe, Emma, and Jax. I appreciate you all and love you all endlessly. I wouldn't be here without you.

Thank you Kristen for your kind words while editing.

Thank you Sara for your constant support, I am so so so thankful to have you on my team.

And thank you, Adam, for always being patient and supportive. For never wavering about this being my job and celebrating the little things with me along the way.

If you enjoyed reading Love at Frost Sight, it would mean the world to me if you would consider leaving a review wherever you like leaving them best. Reviews help indie authors like me grow.

Thank you!
   -Torie Jean

## About the Author

Torie Jean is a granite stater sweating it out in Texas. She is married to her high school sweetheart who reaffirms her belief that the magic of romance is in the tiny everyday things. She has had endometriosis for over half of her life now, and hopes to raise more awareness of the disease with her writing, while providing the happily ever afters people with endo deserve.

instagram.com/authortoriejean

# Also by Torie Jean

*"A heartwarming novel of love triumphing over life's struggles"* - Kirkus Reviews

Finding Gene Kelly - Out Now, on KU, ebook, and in print.

**What's Next?**

Dukes and Dekes - a love letter to Jane Austen and hockey

Coming November 7th, 2023